KT-568-176

FLIES

LITTLE BIRD FLIES

KAREN McCOMBIE

nosy crow

First published in the UK in 2019 by Nosy Crow Ltd
The Crow's Nest, 14 Baden Place
Crosby Row, London, SE1 1YW

Nosy Crow and associated logos are trademarks and/or registered
trademarks of Nosy Crow Ltd

A CIP catalogue record for this book is available from the
British Library.

Printed and bound in Great Britain by Clays Ltd, Elcograf S.p.A.
Typeset by Tiger Media

Papers used by Nosy Crow are made from wood grown in
sustainable forests

ISBN: 978 0 85763 910 3

www.nosycrow.com

FOR MY M –
ONWARDS AND UPWARDS, MY DARLING...
KMcC

"A H-UILE LATHA SONA DHUT,
'S GUN LATHA IDIR DONA DHUT"

"MAY EVERY DAY BE HAPPY FOR YOU,
AND NO DAY EVER BAD"

TORNISH

THE HIGHLANDS
(MAINLAND)

THE ISLE
OF TORNISH,
SCOTLAND,
1861

CHAPTER 1

The dream came to me again.

The one that often wakes me in the grey, pearl light before dawn.

In that quiet time, when only the earliest rising birds shyly begin their songs, I lie, eyes wide, alongside my sleeping sisters in the cramped box bed, my father and brother snoring and snuffling in the small room next door. And always I feel as comforted by my mind's nightly wanderings as if Mother's cool hand had stroked my brow.

But sweet as it is, I have no time to laze and think on my dreamings this morning. Something quite wondrous is happening on the island today and the sudden remembrance of it makes me turn and shake both Ishbel and Effie from their slumbers.

"Wake up! Wake up!" I call out, scrambling and wriggling from between the stirring bodies on either side of me, as if I am some skittish small child instead of a grown girl of twelve.

LITTLE BIRD FLIES

And with much haste and high spirits, we are all soon dressed and fed and about our usual early morning chores. Apart, that is, from Ishbel, who is already gone to the Big House, quite primped and preened, to help with the preparations for the Laird's visitors.

Oh, I cannot wait to see old Mr Menzies' relations! What a thing it is to have fancy folk from a great southern city like London come to our plain little island.

They are taking a Highland tour of course, which is quite the fashion for rich English and Lowland Scots these days, Father says, ever since Queen Victoria herself sang the praises of this northerly part of Scotland. But there must be finer islands for the tourists to see, for none have graced Tornish until now.

So, this day I shall surely always remember, since it is to be unlike all the other *endless* days here that are filled with nothing but chores and school and the same faces whichever way I look, whether they belong to family, neighbours, chickens or cows...

"Again, please!" I hear my younger brother's cries from inside the cottage as Father rattles off a quick trill on his new tin whistle, bought from an Irish pedlar on the mainland this spring.

For a moment, I glance up from the stool I am squatting on here in the dry dirt yard and look at Lachlan and Father through the open front door. They are both infected by the coming day's excitement,

Lachlan jumping around – which risks the fabric of his too-small good jacket splitting, I fear – while Father laughs as he lowers the long whistle from his lips. He is very smart himself in his tweed jacket, waistcoat and trousers. He even had Effie trim his wiry dark-red hair and beard last night. But then we are *all* to look smart today, *all* in our Sunday best though it is the middle of the week.

"*Ist*, now!" says Father, using the short, sharp Gaelic hiss of a word to try to quieten and steady my brother. "You'll hear enough music when Mr Menzies' guests arrive."

Turning back to the wooden bucket wedged between my knees, I find it hard to keep my mind on either the Laird's never-before-sighted relatives or the dishes that need finishing before I change from my work clothes into my good things too.

Instead I idly gaze up at the towering mound of the Glas Crags, which the sun practically perches upon. A yearning to clamber and climb to the very top of the Crags grips me hard; for surely there, at the very summit, so close to the sky and the clouds and the sun itself, I can look out for a distant sighting of the ship! It must be setting off from the mainland soon, and I might see the faintest dot of it, as it begins its slow journey towards our humble harbour.

And with that thought, I am away, as quick and quiet

as I am able. For the short while I am gone, I will not be missed, I tell myself, as the hard, stamped earth of the yard turns to the stubbly long grass that surrounds our cottage and those of the neighbours in our township. Father, Effie and Lachlan; they will perhaps suppose me off at the burn, fetching more water, I persuade myself, as the harsh grass turns to the softer green grazing of the slope, where some cattle idly watch me hurrying by, skirts held high, dirty knees on show.

Now the swoop of soft grass melds into hard, craggy stone dotted with scratchy heather and gorse, and I am breathlessly, happily scampering barefoot from rock to rock, with the sun seeping warm through my unravelling knitted shawl and the rough cloth of my work shirt.

I smile to myself as I gaze up towards the summit of the Crags, the final jags of glinting stone set against the blue summer sky and the white clouds that jostle and tumble over one another.

This far up, the herring gulls caw-caw and whirl around me. It seems the sight of a scrawny girl trying to join them is fine entertainment indeed.

"Little Bird!"

I hesitate for a second at the sound of my name and then turn, neatly, in the narrow path between prickly bundles of gorse bushes, with their strange mix of sun-yellow blossom, fierce thorns and whispers of wool they have stolen from the sheep that have passed this way.

"Am I too fast for you, Will Beaton?" I call down to the boy who has suddenly appeared and now struggles to keep up with me.

"Only here, Bridie MacKerrie," he baits me.

Will is right, of course. On this rocky outcrop of a hill I am like every other person that might come this way. No one can see a limp when every surface is off-kilter and uneven and needs thought. But I have climbed the Crags so often it needs no thought at all.

Just to show Will how sure and fleet I can be, I turn and bound up the last few boulders, to the Glas Crags' highest point; the flat place of stone, with a patched blanket of heather and moss tucked in its crevices.

And ever and always what I see takes my breath away.

Slowly I spin, arms out, and there … *there* is the endless circlet of sea that sways and ebbs around our island, the colour of iron for the most part, merging with an eye-dazzling turquoise on the far shore.

If I let my arms drop and my gaze settle due east, the looming mass of the mainland of Scotland greets me, a ragged jumble of rocks and headlands closest to us, while in the far distance snow-tipped mountains rise towering and immense.

Now I turn around and stare westwards, where the sea has the grand name of the Atlantic Ocean. Its vastness stretches to the horizon … and on and on and *on* it goes till it crashes up against the shores of America.

LITTLE BIRD FLIES

Can you imagine?

It's not just the sea and the far-off land that fill me with wonder. From up here there's the weather to watch too, and the birds swirling and soaring in praise of it or in spite of it.

"I *let* you beat me," says Will, as he finally joins me.

Between gasps, his broad grin shows off the space where a tooth was lost to him years ago, the time he fell on the Crags as we searched about us for gull eggs. I remember that Will and I worried wildly at all the blood. But after we scrambled down from the hill and I washed his face clean at the burn with the corner of my shawl, Will caught sight of himself in the water and could not stop laughing.

And always he is laughing, and always I laugh with him – unless he is taunting me, as he is now.

I am not bothered by Will's teasing. I tease him all the more. For the way his light hair stands up, I am always calling him a thistle-head. And if not that, I tell him often that he is as handsome as the goat his mother keeps, or that even a potato grown on his croft is more bonny than him. Oh yes, Will Beaton might be able to outrun me down on the flat moors, but he can never catch up with my tongue when I let it loose…

"Are you quite well, William?" I ask my friend as his chest heaves from the climb. "The last time I heard a noise like that was when the cow was calving."

Laughter bursts from Will's chest, but I try to keep my countenance and gaze into the newly quiet sky. The gulls are gone – a sea eagle must be about, a winged giant on the hunt for its dinner.

At that thought a shadow passes over me … the sea eagle itself? I spot the flash of fanned white tail and the arc of brown wings as it swoops out across the choppy waters – and I remember I am here to catch a glimpse of the steamship that will bring the Laird's guests.

But alas, the dancing, shifting carpet of silvery waves is still empty.

"So what are you doing up here?" I ask my friend.

"I called by for you, just as your father and Effie and Lachlan were setting off," he tells me. "Your father saw you heading up here. He said he would be grateful if I found you and told you to hurry up!"

"I'll have time enough," I say, smiling at the thought of Father watching me go, and probably rolling his eyes in fond exasperation.

But I don't think Will is listening.

"Ah, see now; John Mackay's boat is at the harbour," I hear him say. "I hope my brother George took his bagpipes with him, for he cannot walk home and back in time to play at the welcome."

"Ha! Well, I suppose the Laird's folk will have to hold their noses while they listen to your brother's reels," I reply merrily, as I consider the London ladies in their dainty muslins and lace, with the smell of the morning's catch in their delicate nostrils.

As I speak, I need not look down towards the harbour; I can very well picture Will's seventeen-year-old brother and John Mackay and the other fishermen landing creels of lobster on the flagstones at the harbour.

And I need not turn as Will is doing now, gauging the distance from the harbour to his own township. For I know that mine is just back down the way we came, ten low cottages nestled together, and that Will's lies further on, tucked into the sandy bay, near the cove where the smaller rowboats are moored. There are two townships more, on the far side of the island, beyond the moor and the lochan and the forest and waterfall. Both face the nothingness of sea, with the promise of an invisible America in the impossible distance.

Should I care to gaze off towards the south of our small island – and I do not – I'd see the woods and the Big House, where the Laird's staff, including my sister Ishbel, will be bustling in readiness for the guests.

I need not gaze down to know that close to the harbour is a little school that stands empty of its pupils today. And close by is the church and its small graveyard, where Mother lies at her rest in the ground, keeping company with the brothers and sisters that never lived long enough for the rest of us to know.

For whenever I am standing here high on the Glas

Crags, I choose not to look at island life below – I know I am peculiar but I prefer to look up and away and beyond…

"Oh!" I gasp, as something so strange happens in that still moment.

Will's hand has brushed against mine!

No – I will not have this. Swiftly, I lift that same hand to my brow and take a few steps forward, making that I am searching for the ship that is not due for two hours at least.

"Little Bird? Bridie?" says Will, not knowing what he has done wrong.

Perhaps he thinks I did not wish him to touch my weakened hand – as if that would bother me! – or perhaps he thinks my cheeks are hot with shyness, that I am coy at the thought of his touch meaning we might one day be sweethearts and not just friends.

But here's the truth that rages in me; instead of shyness, I am full to the brim with a secret that can't be shared or spoken of.

How can I tell Will that it makes me heart-sore to think of Ishbel settling for whichever of the doting, handsome Matheson boys she should prefer (Donal, I am sure), because everyone expects it? Just as they expect fifteen-year-old Effie to marry Will's brother George, by and by?

How can I explain to him that I know neighbours are

already supposing that in a few short years, the pair of *us* will be married and scratching a living from our own croft – and that I shudder when I think of such a thing?

For it is not the future *I* would choose for myself.

Oh yes, my sisters might think themselves blessed to spend all their days on this small patch of rough, grey rock in the choppy, grey sea, because Mother told us so. "Remember, we are the lucky ones," she would say, and talk of the generations of hard-working Highland folk – just like us – who were evicted from their homes over the last hundred years. Father would listen and nod as Mother talked of those cruelly evicted so that their lands could become farms of sheep, with wool that would make the landowning lairds rich. Of ordinary folk whose belongings were cast out on to the road, cottages boarded up, thatched roofs set alight, sometimes with old, bedridden men and women inside!

Like my sisters, I would snivel at the sadness of these terrible truths, while Lachlan drowsed in Mother's arms.

But a quiet, traitorous part of me listened, breath held, to stories of families gathering up their few things and heading for tall ships that would take them to the Carolinas in America, to the wilds of Northern Canada, to Australia and New Zealand on the other side of the earth.

My eyes closed, I would not think of the sorrowful reasons for my fellow Highlanders' leave-takings and loss, but instead let my head fill with wild imaginings. I would yearn, nay, *ache* for such adventure…

For to travel – *that* is the future I would choose for myself, if I *had* a choice. Which of course, as a girl – and one that *some* might think too feeble for the wider world – I do not. But the worst of it is the words Father muttered over Mother's grave, when the earth was but newly patted down.

"Aye, Bridget, you often said we were the lucky ones, and so I shall see to it that myself and the children stay here always."

So there you have it; Father's promise to my dear, dear mother binds me tight to Tornish. And so my raging and restlessness must stay secret and stamped down inside and known to no one.

"Listen, Little Bird," Will says hurriedly, "I didn't mean to—"

"Leave me be for a moment," I murmur, trying to tame my temper.

Safe away from Will, I pick a flat spot a few steps away with a fine mattress of springy moss. I'll lie here for a moment, calming myself with a memory of last night's dream, where my sleeping mind's eye pictured this:

I am standing on the summit of the Glas Crags, bare feet on tiptoes, treading on the soft moss, so close to the sky that I might touch it.

Tilting backwards, arms outstretched, I am caught;

held by a cushioning of air, then borne off by wending winds…

It might well be an unsettling dream to another, but for me the sense of *freedom* it gives me is a joy. And it is a comfort too, because always, *always* as I glide there is a sense of some guiding hand slipping into mine, belonging to someone forever unseen…

"Little Bird?"

Will's voice sounds uncertain; he sounds shy of me.

"What is it?" I answer more kindly, since my mood is not really his fault.

"Is that not the ship…?"

In an instant I sit up. The steamer is not the distant speck I expected to see, but a puffing beast appearing from behind the headland, where its journeying had been obscured.

"It is not meant to arrive at this hour!" I say, as if that changes the fact that a great, steel vessel is thundering its way towards Tornish, which it will reach in no time at all.

Scrabbling to my feet, I walk to the edge of the flat place where Will now stands and join him in staring down towards the harbour. Folk seem to be rushing to join the gathering crowd as news spreads of the ship's approach. In that crowd will be my fluttering sisters, my excitable brother, and my father, no doubt muttering under his breath, hoping that I will not miss this most special occasion.

Wordlessly, Will turns to me and I turn to him.

He grins and I grin back.

"I'll get there first!" I yelp, grabbing hold of my skirt, and seeing in that moment that it is the one with the long tear at the front, with my mended flannel petticoat showing through. My better skirt is folded in the chest at home, alongside the shawl that does not have holes and snags in it.

Ah, the grand folk from London will have to take me as I am, I laugh to myself, as Will and I hurtle down the hill, grabbing stunted tree branches and crackling handfuls of heather to stop ourselves tumbling head over heels.

Secrets, dreams and another sudden torn shred of my skirt; I leave them all behind as I charge towards the harbour and this day I will surely never forget.

CHAPTER 2

At the time of my birth, I arrived like a broken baby bird.

They say I came too soon, born in a bruising storm, instead of waiting a few more weeks for the warming sunshine of spring.

My mother's cries were swallowed up by the winds from the west – from across the sea, from America, I like to think – as they battered and blustered the island, on their way east to wreak havoc on the rest of Scotland.

And then there I was.

"A poor, frail thing you were," Ishbel likes to tell me on winter nights around the fire. "Your chest, it was heaving for breath."

"And your wee foot all twisted," Effie will always add, though she can't truly recall the moment, since she was barely three years old at the time I was born.

Ishbel says Mother and Father thought I'd not last the night. But in the morning I was still there, my good hand clawing the air as if I was desperate to grab hold of life.

When the Laird arrived – with the coins and gifts of fine food and whisky that he always gave his tenants when a child came – my sisters, very young as they were then, proudly ushered him into the cottage.

"And what will you be calling this little scrap, Mr MacKerrie?" the Laird asked Father in English, as he leaned over to study me, bundled cosy inside the wooden crib.

"Bridie, after her mother Bridget, sir," Father answered in English, the sound of the clipped words warmed with the roll and sing of his accent.

"Bridie? Ha! More like birdie. You're just a little bird, aren't you, my dear?" the Laird replied, smiling down at me in delight, my sisters assure me, and I have no doubt of it.

Exhausted as she was, Mother pulled her shawl tight around her and tried to rise from the box bed to properly greet their guest.

"Our girl may not be whole and hearty, sir," she murmured in halting English, "but we will love her as long as we have her."

Mother understood English nearly as well as Father, but stumbled to say the words of that language out loud, as if they were uncomfortable and dry as pebbles in her mouth. And for his part, Mr Menzies spoke mostly English, like all the landowners and rich gentlefolk of

Scotland, but – unlike others of his class – he had an ear keenly tuned to the mother tongue of his tenants.

"Now, please don't rise for *me*, mistress," Mr Menzies told Mother, as he stroked my weak hand and watched my trembling fingers struggle to latch on to one of his. "And don't be offended by my words. The small ones can be fighters. What of the linnet; it is not much bigger than my thumb, yet it soars as well as the buzzard. So this little bird of yours … she may yet fly, eh?"

I will always be grateful to Mr Menzies for trusting in my lust for life.

For here I am, twelve years grown.

Yes, I might be scrawny still, my wings somewhat bent, but I am strong.

And I may be a little bird in name only, but one day, I hope to say goodbye to this island, borne away, as my dream foretells.

One day I *will* fly…

However, this will not be that day. The closest I have come to flying is practically tumbling down the steep side of the Crags with Will.

"How do I look, Little Bird?" he asks now, when we finally stumble and skip towards the back of the milling crowd at the harbour.

The very sound of them stirs the heart; folk clap and stamp along as George – the island's youngest and finest piper – plays a traditional rousing air to welcome the docking ship.

And though I cannot see him yet, I know Father will be tapping his foot, standing alongside the fiddlers with his whistle, in readiness with a tune when George stands down.

What I *can* plainly see is the newly moored steamer, towering over the flat cloth caps of the men and the pretty, crimp-edged, white kerchiefs that the women and many of the younger girls wear.

"You look fine," I turn and answer my friend, and begin straightening his cap and plucking sprigs of heather from the good jumper that Mistress Beaton just knitted him. "But keep your arm across the front so your mother doesn't see the hole there…"

I don't ask Will how *I* look, because I know that I must seem like some savage child that has been living wild on the moor!

Will has no idea why I am laughing, but joins in anyway, all the while returning the favour and brushing away grasses and twigs and blossom that have stuck to me.

But we both stop laughing when we see Effie's furious face. My middle sister might be talked of as pretty, having the rich red hair of Father, and apple cheeks in her soft, round face, but her prettiness is all too often disguised by all the scowling she does. She is like one of the cattle of a summer's evening when the midges are biting and maddening them.

Now a smile slips unbidden on to my face, as I imagine fiery-haired Effie as Mr Menzies' prized shaggy, red Highland cow, the one that stands out among the rest of the bulky black herd.

It is not a wise thing to do, of course. Effie – in her best skirt and her new-made checkered plaid shawl – steps straightaway from her friends and comes over to berate me.

"What humours you so, Bridie? Does it amuse you that you are to shame Father today? Where have you been? Why did you not go home and change into your good clothes?"

Her words come fast as they often do, allowing me no time to answer. Not that I have an answer that will suit her. The fact of it is, I never have an answer for *either* of my bossy sisters, who – without our mother with us – see it as their job to chide and order me around, as much as they pet and adore Lachlan.

"Yes, but it is the fault of the visitors for coming early," says Will, trying to protect me. "You see, Little Bird—"

"For heaven's sake, her name is *Bridie*, Will Beaton!" snaps Effie. "How many times have you been told over the years?"

Ah, but since we were both young children, Will has always mimicked Mr Menzies in calling me Little Bird, in English. Even Mother – who held on to her Gaelic like a treasure – would smile fondly when she heard Will call me so. Perhaps it amused her to hear such unnatural English words spring forth from the mouth of an islander child, or perhaps it was because Little Bird translated to Gaelic as "*bìgein-Brìghde*", meaning "St Brìghde's little bird", the very name for a linnet.

But it is not just the English of my pet name that Effie dislikes. It is the fact that both Effie *and* Ishbel rail against this pet name itself. They worry that people hearing it will think of me as small and to be pitied. But I don't think folk do pity me, and anyway, I don't *care* if they do. I was born into this body and know no other. And if I can manage what everyone else can – even if it sometimes happens a little slower – then what of it?

"And the mess of your hair!" Effie turns back to me and sighs. "When Ishbel sees she will give me such trouble for not making sure that you were decent!"

To think of Effie getting a scolding from our eldest sister causes another smile to slip on to my face. At seventeen, Ishbel is only two years Effie's senior, but being a maidservant for the Laird gives her airs and graces indeed.

"What *is* this!"

At those words my straggly long black hair is near pulled clean from my head.

Ishbel is not one for nagging chatter like hot-headed

Effie. Her scorn is shown by a disapproving and quiet coolness.

"Effie, could you not have tied a simple braid for Bridie?" I hear Ishbel address our sister sharply, and straightaway feel her tug my grass-matted hair into something less like a broom that's been sweeping leaves from the door.

Ishbel's hair is as black as mine, but is pinned low around her head in shiny coils, the like of which any fine young lady of importance might be proud. She has worn it that way ever since Father took her to the far-off town on the mainland to buy food and cloth stuffs last year, where he said he caught her studying the fashions of a group of English ladies on their Grand Tour.

"Ow!" I yelp, as the tugging cricks at my neck.

"*Bidh thu slàn mus pòs thu…*" Ishbel grumbles as she grapples with my knots and tangles.

And then I feel my sister hesitate. "*You'll be whole by the time you marry*"… it's a common thing for mothers of the island – of all the Gaelic-speaking places, I suppose – to say to their whining daughters as they drag a comb or brush through their fresh-washed hair. I've always supposed it to mean that hair would grow back by and by; that it's best to be patient and not moan.

I remember Mother laughingly saying those very words to us three girls often enough. Is Ishbel remembering too? Perhaps I should say some—

"OW!" I yelp louder, as Ishbel starts back at her task anew.

"For shame, Bridie!" she snaps at me. "Some things you must just bear."

And that sums up Ishbel; she is tall and slight as a sapling, carrying herself with such serious forbearance, resigned to her lot and considering everyone foolish who does not think the way *she* does.

In fact, not so long ago, Father proclaimed – to Ishbel's great pleasure – that she was like a stone statue he'd seen in a book, of some Greek goddess or another. Grand and queenly she was, Father said, with her chin held high and such a certainty about her. Well, the only certainty right now is that Ishbel is practically pulling the hair out of my head.

"Be still, Bridie, or I'll—"

Ishbel's warning is lost as cheers go up.

I don't care whether my hair is tidy or raggedy; feeling her grip relax a little, I seize my opportunity and pull away from Ishbel's hold, running from both her and Effie and their glowering. Hurrying forward, I sneak through the crowd – sure that Will cannot be far behind – so that I might see these grand folk from London at last...

And there they are, two men in long, thick coats and similarly patterned checkered trousers, with grey top hats and silver-tipped canes. Unlike the bearded men of

Tornish, they wear just moustaches, but quite twirled at each end! They stride confidently off the steamer's ramp to shake hands with the Laird, and make some small talk. They also nod at the musicians, some in kilts, within whose number stands, of course, George Beaton playing his pipes, Fergus and Donal Matheson with their fiddles, and my father holding his tin whistle, Lachlan crouched proudly at his feet.

"Well, you two," says a warm voice beside me. "What do you think to our visitors?"

I have found myself by Mistress Beaton. She takes care of the old Laird's washing, drying his bed linen and clothing on lines by the seashore, so that the Big House must always be filled with the fresh salty spice of the ocean.

"I think they look very smart!" I say, my heart surging with the excitement of having strangers from the outside world touch down on our shores.

"Have you found out who these kin are to Mr Menzies, Mother?" Will asks, catching me up.

"The first gentleman is the son of a long-dead cousin of the Laird, it seems," says Mistress Beaton, with some satisfaction at knowing this detail. "I think the second gentleman is a friend, accompanying the family."

I am listening keenly to Mistress Beaton's words, at the same time as straining to watch the gentlemen turn their attention back towards the boat, holding their hands so that the ladies – oh, the fine ladies! – may descend safely from the ramp and on to dry land. The first two to step ashore wear bright-coloured dresses that puff out so, with many layers of fine cotton petticoats underneath their braid-edged skirts. With ruffles of intricate lace rippling softly at their wrists and necks, I feel I am looking at wondrous birds of paradise from the far Indies.

It gives me pleasure to see that one is quite young, perhaps the same age as Effie. I wonder, might I sometime be able to approach and talk to her during her visit? I would *so* like to hear what it is like to travel the whole length of the country in a steam train! What a strange affair that must be. My, she must have seen such things in her life: the sights and sounds of London, and of Glasgow too, where the train terminated. And on that journey alone, what wonders of towns and villages and valleys and hills did she see?

Oh, I know that in many places it might not be natural for a young lady of *her* kind to converse with a girl of *my* type, but the Laird is not a man to stand on ceremony. I am already a favourite of Mr Menzies', so perhaps he might think to introduce me to her…?

"What is this about?" I hear Will mutter in confusion, and switch my glance to a lady who now follows, in such a strange guise! After a moment's surprise, I guess it to be full black mourning, from dress to cape, from gloves to lace veil. I have heard that this is done, but never seen such a thing. This woman — a widowed grandmother perhaps? — reminds me of the crows that make the thick woods behind the Big House their shaded home. And aiding her is a maidservant, holding her elbow. Though it seems to me the maid is being a little rough with the old lady…

I am staring so hard at this odd pairing that it takes me a moment to see that I am *also* being stared at.

The younger of the ladies in layers and lace is casting her eyes over me in a way that makes me see quite clear how I am to her.

A peasant girl in torn and tatty clothes.

A child with a bent foot and one arm weak and withered.

She sees all that is me and sees no one of worth.

The warmth of day leaves me as a brisk wind lifts off the sea and bites to my core.

CHAPTER 3

Flutter and flap, flutter and flap.

The wet cotton I'm hanging slaps against the breeze, like a rhythm you could sing to. I toss the dancing hair from my face and begin to hum.

"Are you listening to me, Bridie?" scolds Effie.

"No," I mutter, so she can't hear me.

My sister is always telling me something. Some way I should behave, some chore I should have done differently, some story that turns into a lesson I'm meant to heed.

"After you've finished here, you'll need to fetch the water," Effie orders, as if I didn't know that I must. As if I hadn't already been to the burn and brought back two buckets of clean, cold water. If she bothered to look she'd see the early sun turning the wet of my skirts to clouds of steam.

Folk might think I have been set ablaze, I think, as I look down at the damp mess of myself and laugh.

"Bridie! This is no time for foolishness. Everything

must be done well today. You wouldn't want Father shamed of our home, or old Mr Menzies shamed of us all, would you?"

"Effie, the Laird's London visitors will not care about our home!" I say, knowing I should stop there, but I don't. "The cows could be sitting inside our cottage, having some broth and a chat, and those fancy folk would know nothing of it."

Effie's nostrils flare at my mocking, like a stag about to charge. Perhaps I'm lucky that she has thick red braids about her head and not antlers.

"Bridie, you know Father said Mr Menzies will no doubt take them for some air now that they are rested from their travels yesterday. And as *our* township is the closest to the Big House, his visitors may well—"

A sharp whistle bursts through the air, and I spin around at the sound of it.

It's Will.

Just the sight of my friend gladdens my heart; he has rescued me.

"Little Bird!" Will calls. "Are you coming to spy on the English visitors with me afore school?"

"No, she is not!" Effie answers for me, as she shoos him away like some daft chicken trying to roost on our mantleshelf among the ornaments.

"Oh, yes I *am*," I reply, fastening the final piece of washing, and knowing my work is done. I tuck my unkempt black hair behind my ears and go after Will.

It's true that yesterday's sighting of Mr Menzies' guests left me with a sour taste in my mouth, but perhaps I was being unfair to them, especially the staring, unsmiling girl. Perhaps she was tired after such a long journey. She may have been seasick for all I know, like lads are when they first go on the fishing boats. And perhaps in my messy, torn state I reminded her of some destitute London street child, instead of just a careless girl that forgot herself.

"What am I to do with you, Bridie MacKerrie?" Effie shouts after me.

"Nothing," I laugh in reply. "There's nothing to be done with me! I'm fine as I am."

And I'm off along the path in the rough grass worn by the cattle's feet.

"What is she bothering about?" asks Will, holding a hand out to me as I catch him up and go to leap the wee burn.

Yes, I might've almost stumbled a little there, but I have no need of his help. Will should know better; I can manage. I always do.

"Effie and Ishbel are like hens with new feed, they are so excited about these visitors," I say, ignoring his hand and grabbing up my skirts instead, to better find my footing.

Ishbel was very particular about her appearance this

morning when she rose, spending so long at Mother's mirror braiding and coiling her hair before slipping on her intricately crimp-edged cap that she was almost late setting off for the Laird's house. As if his visitors will be interested in a girl who will be lugging their coals and cleaning their chamberpots for them!

Though I admit I am afire to take a closer look at these people; to gawp at their wealth and finery, perhaps to see the girl or her widow-woman grandmother in her crow's mourning.

"Bridie! Bridie, wait for me!" comes a reedy voice behind us.

"Ah, we have our shadow with us today." Will grins at me, showing off the gap where his front tooth should be.

"Indeed," I sigh, though I am not wont to grumble when Lachlan seeks out our company. He has precious little of his own, unless you count the very youngest children of the township or the animals in our keep. The boys around his own age have little time for him. At eight years old he is as clever as any of them, *cleverer* in fact, and sweeter too, but he will not join in their rough-and-tumble and that confounds them. He is like a skinny-legged lamb, barely able to keep its balance as fledgling goats batter and ram each other in jest.

"Where have you sprung from?" I ask him, as he catches us up, and finds his shoulders a resting place for Will's arm.

"I was making an eel!" Lachlan says excitedly. "I took some hair from the tail of the black-and-tan pony and have weighted it down in the stream with a stone. How long do you think it will take to be changed?"

Will and I smile over Lachlan's head. It's an old practice the children tell each other of. Left in the water of the burn, over time, slime will attach to the hair, and sure enough it looks as if an eel is wriggling in the ripples.

"A long while. You must be patient," I tell my brother, rubbing my knuckles through his scrubby mess of red hair.

It's not just the children who tell him tales like these. The worst is Effie; she is in thrall to all the old superstitions. She will happily sit of an evening at the fire, telling Lachlan wonder tales of the fairies and the Little Folk and Brownies that make mischief, turning milk sour and cattle skittish and all manner of nonsense.

"Where are you and Will headed, Bridie?" my brother asks, blinking from one to the other of us. "Are you not going to school today?"

He sounds hopeful. Clever as he is, Lachlan hates school. He has all the correct answers in his head and can say them clear enough, but ask him to write and it is as if all reason is stuck somewhere between his head and his hand. Nothing comes but a scrawl. It is because by nature, he leans towards writing with his

left hand. Which is incorrect, according to Mr Simpson
the schoolmaster. He lets Lachlan know this over and
over again, by smacking his clutched hands with a cane
in front of the whole class, and by rapping Lachlan's
knuckles with a thick wooden ruler in between times.

"We *are* going to school," I tell him, ignoring his
grumbles of disappointment, "but first we are off to see
if we can catch ourselves sight of the gentlemen and
ladies that are staying with Mr Menzies…"

The great, grey, weathered building that is the Laird's
house – it rises up in front of us now, its many gleaming,
glinting windows winking in the sunlight. They are so
numerous that I have lost count of them whenever I
have walked around the outside of the house, while
waiting for Ishbel to finish her work (and perhaps give
me some small leftover from the kitchen), or during
those long weeks when I was young and kept Father
company while he rebuilt the crumbling wall around
the gardens, to keep the deer from Mr Menzies' bonnie
flowerbeds.

"It is so tall!" murmurs Lachlan, wondering – as he
always does – at the marvel of a building that can be
three floors high, when the newer cottages and older
blackhouses of the island are hunkered down low to the
ground so that the almost constant winds rush smoothly
over them.

The Big House is old too, though not from antiquity,

like the ancient standing stones on the moor. Mr Menzies once told me it is a hundred years old and more, built in 1750, by some distant kin of his. There is a portrait of this kinsman on the wall within the house, Ishbel says, along with many other dark, dour, unsmiling people, who cannot surely be related to Mr Menzies, who is *always* smiling, even though he is white-haired and has no wife and children for company. The Laird has often told Father that he has company enough with the books in his library and the kindness and conversation of the decent folk that make up his staff and tenants.

"Never a better man," Father often says of Mr Menzies.

And what would Father say now, if he saw the three of us begin scrambling over the back wall of the Big House, like troublemaking urchins? I hope he would roar in amusement, as he does when we tell him of the trees we've climbed and the waterfalls we've ducked, shrieking, under. Or the game with the rowing boats at the cove, where we've jumped from one to the other and someone *always* tumbles into the shallows and cannot get themselves up and out of the waves for laughing.

As we settle ourselves down on the top of the wall, like three curious, head-tilting sparrows, Mistress Matheson – who cooks and keeps house for the Laird – comes huffing and puffing to the open kitchen door. Fergus and Donal's mother is a big, comely woman, always ruddy of cheek, but today her face is roast-red as she rubs a hand against her sweating brow. And then she catches sight of we three and seems to brighten.

"Bridie!" she cries. "Just the girl! Can you come help me?"

I jump down off the wall and hurry over to her as she disappears back into the kitchen, pausing only to quickly turn and shrug my shoulders at Will and Lachlan.

The three of us are not the only ones who are confused; as soon as I step into the kitchen – the only room in the Big House I have ever been in – I see the deep frown on my sister's face.

"You cannot send her up!" she is saying to a clearly agitated Mistress Matheson, while waving a bloody knife in one hand and a neatly skinned rabbit in the other.

"Well, what am I to do? We are too busy here to run errands!" counters Mistress Matheson, waving at the table heaving with food, while pots hiss and spit at the range.

"Is everything all right?" I ask warily.

"No, it is not," Mistress Matheson replies. "The gentlemen will take their breakfast shortly. But the *ladies* do not rise till late morning and will breakfast then. Though a tray must be taken to *one* of the ladies who does not choose to eat with the family –"

With that, Mistress Matheson hands me a tray with a small plate of thin-cut bread and butter and a china cup of tea on it.

"– and if *that* is not enough, the lawyer gentleman staying complains that he has a chip in his shaving bowl and requires a new one!"

"But I cannot … I must get to school," I mumble shyly, as Mistress Matheson dives into a dresser and begins a clanking search – for a suitable shaving bowl, I suppose.

"Of course you can, Bridie," Ishbel says with a weary sigh. "Go out into the corridor and you'll see the back stairs. The lady is on the floor above, the first door you come to. Knock and wait; I think she is dressing, so the ladies' maid will no doubt answer. Go, quick!"

And so I take my leave, knowing I must hurry but treading up the cold, narrow, dark staircase so very carefully, scared that my shaking hands will spill the precious cargo. At last, I reach the first floor and push a door open with my shoulder – and stare in surprise at the length of the corridor I find myself in. It is panelled in some fine polished wood, and is longer by far than our whole cottage!

I want to stare longer, or to tip toe the length of the soft-looking patterned rug that snakes along the landing, but I must not. Balancing the tray on my stronger hand, I use my weaker to gently knock on the nearest door.

At a loss as to what to say to the sour-faced maid I saw at the harbour yesterday, I am even more at a loss for words when the door is drawn open – and the Black

Crow herself peers out at me!

For the first moment, I am struck by the fact that this woman is so deep in mourning that she wears her veil indoors. A moment more and I am struck by the intricate lacework of the veil itself; it is so very fine, roses and vines entwined.

Then a glint of eyes peering back at me from under the dark garden of stitch-work is the undoing of me.

"Your breakfast!" I gabble, placing the tray down on the floor and running back the way I came, as if I had just encountered a sprite in disguise.

Pattering madly down the stairs, my bare feet land at last on the cool, smooth flagstone of the passageway on the ground floor. Instantly, the very coldness of it stills me, bringing me to my senses.

I smooth my skirts and my hair, take a deep breath, and prepare to walk back into the kitchen and show my sister that I can handle myself quite well, in fact.

But before I do so, I see that the door to the right, one that I suppose would lead into the main house, is half open. Mistress Matheson will be expecting me back, of course, but oh, now that I am here – further inside the house than I have ever been – I would *so* like to see what lies beyond this door, to perhaps just catch a glimpse of the stern-faced portraits in the grand hall.

I step closer and peer through the gap – then pull myself back in haste as soon as I see someone has had the same idea. The two gentlemen guests are perusing the paintings closely.

"I suppose you'll ask him after dinner this evening?" I hear one say.

"Indeed. Though looking at this place, I wonder that Menzies will have any money to lend me," the other voice replies bleakly. "Unless these paintings are worth something. What do you think, Jenkins?"

"I don't think *anything* is worth much here," says the other. Then he says some English words I am not sure of, before I catch some I *do* know. "Why would the old man not think to turn to sheep-farming? That's where the money lies!"

"Sheep? Urgh," groans the other voice. "How I would hate to be surrounded by such stupid creatures."

"But is the old man not already surrounded by stupid creatures, and ones that make him *less* money?"

It takes just a second for me to be sure I understood the meaning of that; that both men are now laughing at we islanders, and I think I must gasp too loud in shock. For next I hear an odd noise; a tappiting sound that is coming this way fast – now accompanied by a sharp barking.

"Come back here, damn you!" I hear one of the men roar as I run clean through the kitchen, ignoring Ishbel's puzzled stare.

Clearing the yard in no time at all, I scramble up the

wall and sit astride it so fast that you would never know I am weaker than most.

I'm about to tell Will and Lachlan to jump over the other side with me when Lachlan cries out in delight.

"Look, it's a dog, Bridie!" he yelps, as a creature dashes out of the kitchen doorway and stops dead at the sight of us. Its hair is as scruffy as Lachlan's but the colour of sand, with a hand-sized "saddle" of brown fur on its back. Small as it is, this little pup has a bark as loud as a hound six times its size.

"Patch! Patch, come here at once, you little devil…" a man's voice growls just as fiercely, and one of the men of the visiting party comes barging out of the back door. He is wearing a dark-green tweed sporting suit and brandishing a polished stick I had not noticed in my brief sighting of him in the hallway. Does he … does he mean to use it on the dog if it does not obey his order?

"No, NO!" shouts Lachlan, and jumps down off the wall, certain too that the angry gentleman is about to cause his dog harm.

And then what am I to do, but jump *back* down from the wall to make sure no harm comes to my brother in turn? Alas, I land awkwardly on my twisted foot, and my limp is more acute and slows me down, so that the man has tight hold of Lachlan's skinny arm before I know it.

"Let him go!" I order the so-called gentleman.

"Let him go? You are trespassing on your master's private property and you ask that I should let this rascal *go*?" bellows the man, who seems no gentleman to me, however well dressed he is.

"Now then, what's to do?" I hear a familiar voice call out, and am relieved to see Mr Menzies come around from the direction of the stables to join us.

He is not the only one; coming out of the back door of the house is the other gentleman, Ishbel and Mistress Matheson in their aprons, wondering what all the commotion is about. Ishbel's hands cover her mouth, alarmed by the sight of her sister and brother railing against someone they should not.

"These scoundrels have entered your grounds, sir, and I'm about to rid them for you," says the man in his clipped English voice, so different from the soft rolling voices of the Highlands. He talks as if we are vermin, about to be routed and clubbed!

"Mr Menzies, sir," Will bursts in, appearing at my side. "You know we meant no harm. We were just—"

"Just paying me a visit, I'm sure," Mr Menzies interrupts good-naturedly, especially now he sees the bouncing dog jump up affectionately at Lachlan's legs. Gently, he pats a hand on Lachlan's shoulder in such a way that lets the sour-faced man know he needs to release his grip. I am relieved to see him do so.

"Children, this is Mr Palmer-Reeves, my late cousin's

son, who has brought with him his family and his friend Mr Jenkins," says Mr Menzies, indicating the man in the doorway, who is smirking now, highly entertained by the goings-on. "They have come to see our sweet island home, as part of their tour of the Highlands."

The Laird says that so kindly, which makes me angry for the easy way his guests seemed to mock his hospitality when I overheard them inside.

But all I can do, *must* do, is give a reluctant curtsey, and the boys give a brisk bow, before Mr Menzies continues with his introductions.

"And this fine fellow is Patch, a cairn terrier," Mr Menzies adds, for the benefit of my brother.

Lachlan manages a small smile, though he is rubbing at the place where his arm was so tightly squeezed.

"Mr Palmer-Reeves, this strapping young fellow is Will, brother of George Beaton, who piped you off the steamer yesterday," the Laird continues with his cheerful introductions. "And Little Bird – I mean, *Bridie* – and young Lachlan here are the children of a very dear friend of mine, Robert MacKerrie, master stone-mason, a piper and musician himself, and one of the elders among my tenants here on Tornish."

A fine speech the Laird has made, but all the time this Mr Palmer-Reeves has a look on his face as if the manure stack by the stables is troubling him.

"Bridie!" Ishbel suddenly calls out sharply. "The

school bell will be ringing any time now. Off with you all!"

She flaps her apron at us, shooing us away before we cause any more bother.

"Aye, off with you," smiled Mr Menzies. "And we'll see you later, I think, for a little celebration of Beltane?"

"Yes, sir," I say to Mr Menzies in Gaelic, with another little curtsey, at the same time grabbing my brother by the shoulder of his jumper and dragging him away from the tongue-lolling dog whose head he's scratching.

Quickly, myself, Lachlan and Will hurry off towards the wall, which we scramble up, the crevices providing perfect stepping places for our bare toes and handholds for our roughened fingers.

At the top, with one leg slung over, I turn my head quickly, scraping back a long, fluttering piece of hair that's wrapping my neck like a scarf of black wool.

It seems that as we three take our leave, we are being most keenly watched.

By Mr Menzies, with a cheery smile.

By Ishbel, biting her lip, and Mistress Matheson, flapping her flour-covered hand in farewell.

By Mr Palmer-Reeves, "gentleman", whose moustachioed scowl is something to see.

By a small dog, with a stumpy wagging tail – till a sideways kick with a polished boot shushes him.

By a black figure in an upstairs window, who leaps

back as if scalded when she sees that I've spied her.

I shudder, though I know not if it is because of the scowling or being the focus of the Black Crow.

More likely it is because I can clearly hear the dull *ding-a-ding* of the school bell and can already feel the sharp smart of Mr Simpson's cane on my hand for being late...

CHAPTER 4

It is good to see Lachlan happy, after his day of caning and shaming.

And being made to stand in the corner for the ink blots that spoiled his scrawled work.

It is good that we are all having a ceilidh this first day of May, Beltane, where we celebrate the spring and the blessed summer to follow.

In Mother's childhood, and her mother's before that, and childhoods of mothers for centuries back, Beltane was a time of superstition and tradition entwined, of earnest wishes made to keep cattle safe and crops growing.

I do not know how it is celebrated in other far-flung places of the Highlands and islands now, if it is at all, but here on Tornish it is a time of entertainment for the islanders, young and old. Most from the other townships have come this fair, warm early evening to the gentle, grassy slope that sits at the foot of the Glas Crags.

Effie and I are at the top of the slope now, along

with Lachlan and some twenty or so of the younger children.

At the bottom, where the slope becomes meadow, older folk sit on chairs brought out from the nearby houses of our township for their ease. They catch up on news, and tap their feet to the reels the menfolk are playing on their fiddles.

The older girls and boys are talking too, but with eyes that sparkle and smiles that say more than their words do. (Ishbel has to content herself with the looks and smiles that Donal Matheson throws her as he fiddles alongside his brother.)

But that is not *everyone* who is here. Down below, watching the festivities, is the Laird, which is to be expected. But he has his visitors with him, which casts a gloom on this bright Beltane evening…

"Why must *they* come?" I say, standing with my hands on my hips as I glower down at Mr Palmer-Reeves and his finely feathered, proud-faced flock. Though one face I cannot make out, since it is covered in a black veil.

I know I am being unfair, and Mother would chide me for it. For just as I cannot take against all cattle, simply because one cow kicked me when I was milking her last summer, I should not take against the visiting womenfolk, just because I dislike the so-called gentlemen in their party, both of whom mock the Laird, while one presumes to borrow money from him.

43

"And why must you speak English when you are with me?" Effie answers my question with one of her own, as she loosens the knot in her bundled apron, which holds the still-warm Beltane bannocks she has baked and brought here for the children now clamouring around us.

It is not worth answering that question; I often do not know when I am speaking either the Gaelic of home or the English of school. Mother didn't like for us to slip into English either, but Father says English is something all us islanders must embrace, so that if the need comes, we can make our way in the world. Of course, when Father talks of the "world", he is talking of the mainland. And those that might go will mostly be the island *boys*, who – like many of the menfolk – go to the mainland for extra work in lean years.

The girls of Tornish never go far.

And because of Father's promise to Mother, we MacKerrie girls will *certainly* never go far.

We will never see marvels like sky-high bridges made of iron, or curiosities like Irish pedlars selling arrays of wares, such as the tin whistle Father bought himself before returning to us from a trip to Oban.

My sisters and I are expected to marry and make do and *stay*.

"Here, take one!" says Effie, holding up the corners of her apron so as to make a cloth bowl of the bannocks.

LITTLE BIRD FLIES

The words are barely flown from her lips when many small hands reach and scramble for one of the round breads that Effie has marked with a cross on one side, especially for Beltane. "And mind, roll them gently. It is unlucky to have one that breaks, or that lands cross-side up!"

"You'll put the fear in them, Effie," I admonish her, thinking that there may be whoops and skirls of laughter now, but there'll be tears before long from those little children who find their bannock torn open or marked-side up at the bottom of the grassy slope.

"It is what it is," Effie says, echoing the words our mother would say, whether she was talking of a bloodied knee one of us would weepily present to her, a bad summer harvest or the wasting cough that came to take her from us three years since. "Will you be wanting one, Bridie?"

Of course I will have one. I may not hold with the superstitions Effie loves so dear, but I am always happy to fill my belly. So I quickly hold out my hand for the bannock my sister is offering me – and hear her gasp at the weeping red weals of my palm.

"Mr Simpson did this?" she asks, though she knows my answer is to be yes. No one else but the schoolteacher has an instrument so thin and harsh and takes such pleasure in using it. "Let me see your other hand…"

I lift the arm that is weak, and see tears prickle in

Effie's eyes as she beholds the marks on my withered hand.

That irks me; I will not have pity. To use her words and Mother's, my hand *is what it is* and serves me well enough. I am about to whip it away from her gaze when she lets go an apron corner, allowing the leftover bannocks to tumble, and wraps both her hands around mine, rubbing them as if her care will make the weals disappear.

"Oh, listen, George has heard news that will cheer you," Effie says as she rubs, making my heart quicken. "A fisherman from the mainland says that Mr Simpson is leaving the parish. He is to take himself off to Australia for a new life!"

Ah, my heart heaves with joy – to be free of our schoolteacher is a Beltane blessing indeed! But behind the joy, my dark secret burbles and belches, turning the joy sour. For I suddenly ache to have the freedom that Mr Simpson has lying yawning before him for the taking…

"Does that not please you, Bridie?" Effie says, frowning a little, not understanding why a shadow has passed across my eyes.

"It does, it does indeed!" I tell her, pushing the searing jealousy away and forcing myself to smile. "Now, shall we do as Lachlan and the others have done and roll our bannocks?"

Effie's face lights up in a wondrous, childlike way, banishing for once her tight, often-cross countenance. For a moment, I recognise the dear playmate she was to me, before Mother left us. Her hands suddenly dropping away from my fingers, she cries, "*Mine* will reach the bottom first!"

And with that, she bends and scoops a fallen bannock, rolling it after the children that are already lowping and shrieking their way down the slope towards the music and the gathering below.

I grab another discarded bannock and toss it too, scampering down the hill in a zigzagging style – like the scuttle of a crab, Will calls it – so as to keep my balance.

A breathless few moments later the ground beneath my bare feet flattens out, and I toss the hair away from my face the better to see where my bannock has settled.

But what I see is a company of children standing so forlorn, staring down at the ground as if they are beholding some terrible misfortune.

"Bridie!" Lachlan calls out to me. "The bannocks, they are *all* broken or crossed, every one of them!"

"Every one of them…" Effie repeats his words in dark wonder, as two of the littlest girls cling to her skirts and snivel. "This is a bad omen, is it not?"

"This is simply bread, is it not," I retort sharply, keen to quell the rising emotion I sense growing.

"Little Bird is right," says Mr Menzies, joining us with his warm smile and his arms wide, as if appealing for calm. "This is just bread, and this is just a game, a jest."

"What is happening here?" says a soft, high voice, and I turn to see we are joined by the girl, Mr Palmer-Reeves' daughter.

This close, I have the scent of her; a piercing, sweet smell, like some kind of perfumed flower. The bonnet she wears, made of a brushed felt the colour of buttermilk, is dotted with clusters of cloth roses. Beneath its brim, perfect curls of golden hair frame her face. I think she might be the most remarkable thing I have ever come across, and I instantly regret the fleeting bitter thoughts I entertained at the top of the slope.

"Ah, Miss Kitty," says the Laird, bending to pick up a bannock, "you see before you a very old tradition the children enjoy. *Most* of the time!"

Miss Kitty? I roll the English name around in my head and decide I like the trill of it.

"My!" says Miss Kitty, blinking at the bannock the Laird has passed to her. "How very ... silly!"

With that, her gloved fingers daintily drop the bannock to the ground as if she'd been given a cowpat to hold. And in that instant I realise this Miss Kitty *is* remarkable – remarkable in her likeness to her awful, grasping father.

"Oh!" murmurs Mr Menzies, taken aback. "Well!

Um, well, I think it is perhaps time we made merry and danced… Here, Little Bird, I'll take you for my partner in this jig!"

I know that I am a favourite of the Laird's, and I am happy for that, and happy to be this generous gentleman's partner. Happy to walk towards the dancers on his arm as the rude, golden-haired girl watches.

At a wave from Mr Menzies, the musicians play louder and faster and I am pulled into a sudden crowd of dancers, skipping and spinning and tossing skirts around me.

"Bravo, Little Bird!" Mr Menzies laughs and claps his hands, as I skip and spin and toss my skirts with the best of them.

From the corner of my eye I see that Miss Kitty and her party are all staring at us with faint disgust, as if faced with some drab herd of beasts in a zoological menagerie.

But I choose to care not. Encouraged by the Laird's applause, I do another full spin. And yet, though it is done at speed, with my skirt and petticoat fanning around me, I have the strangest sensation.

It is as if all around me the world is quite slowed. Slowed enough to note clearly the faces of the people around me, young and old, musician and dancer, crofter and visitor.

Each one portrays *such* an expression of surprise! But

wait; it is more than that, much more. It is horror.

And as my oddly torpid circling spins me back around to face my partner in the jig, I see what this horror is about.

At my feet lies the Laird, groaning, clutching his chest.

In a lightning moment, Father and the other elders rush to his aid, and I am jostled this way and that, like seaweed in the current.

"What is happening? What is wrong with him?" Mr Palmer-Reeves bellows, hurrying towards the throng of helpers.

I see Father slowly rise, tears clearly visible in his blue eyes.

"It is no use, sir," Father says in English.

For a moment my muddled mind is fixed in Gaelic and does not listen clearly to the meaning of what Father has said. Or maybe it is because I cannot trust that I *do* understand it, not when I see Mr Palmer-Reeves' reaction. For what decent man would turn to his family and raise his eyebrows, as if he has just heard some surprisingly good news?

And what wife and child, along with a lawyer friend of supposed high standing, would return similar looks – or even risk a small, victorious smile, as Miss Kitty has just done?

Only the grandmother, the Black Crow, seems to sway and need steadying by her maid. Though what odd emotion might have caused that, I do not care to guess at, for I trust none in that party to have a normal, decent human feeling.

But my gaze is torn from the loathsome visitors when I see the other elders follow Father's lead, rising forlornly to their feet and pulling the caps from their bowed heads.

It is then that poor Mr Menzies is visible to me again. He is lying straight and still, his wise old eyes wide open, though they see nothing of the blue sky above him.

A stunned moment of silence hangs over the gathered islanders, before the waves of grief that are sure to come.

And in that moment, I swear that all the birds of Tornish cry out in a chorus of sorrow and loss.

This Little Bird tilts her head back, opens her throat and joins them.

CHAPTER 5

The rain has pummelled down all day.

Heavy sheets of it fell on the long slow funeral procession.

It drummed steadily on the roof of the packed little church during the service, practically drowning out the sweet Gaelic hymns Mr Menzies always found so moving.

And at the graveside, it matched the flowing tears and quickly turned the earth to a sludge of mud around our feet.

It hammers down still, now on the patiently standing men in the yard of the Big House.

"Ishbel?" I whisper, since it is a day for low voices. "Why does he leave them this way?"

The "he" I speak of is Mr Palmer-Reeves, who Father and the other island elders are awaiting, so that they can pay their respects.

"Perhaps he knows nothing of our ways," says Ishbel, straightening the dry skirt I have brought her, so that she does not walk through the corridors of the house with the mud-soaked one she wore to the funeral earlier.

I stare out of the window at Father and the men, who are posed like steady soldiers, silent, eyes front, hands clasped in front of them, acting as if they are unaware of the rain that runs down their necks and drips from their beards. Whatever my sister says, I cannot think that paying respects is a tradition that is not understood in a worldly place such as London, where Mr Palmer-Reeves hails from. Where I wish he would return to.

"Shouldn't someone tell him they are there?" I beseech her.

I see Ishbel and Mistress Matheson exchange looks.

"Mr Palmer-Reeves knows full well that they stand there," Ishbel says, her cheeks looking more hollow than usual.

"And he chooses instead to drink whisky and smoke cigars and have a fine old time with that lawyer friend of his," grumbles Mistress Matheson, gazing out worriedly at her own soaked husband.

"Well, I think they cannot call themselves gentlemen," I mutter blackly.

"It is not your place to think any such thing," Ishbel says angrily, as she ties a fresh apron around her waist. "We have a new Laird and we must just bear it."

A rage boils within me, for I do not know how I *can* bear it. This time last week, I was tearing down the side of the Glas Crags, my heart soaring with possibilities, expecting a day I would never forget. How could I know it was to be the first day when the island would change for the worse?

"Listen, while you're here, Bridie, will you go upstairs and fetch something?" says Mistress Matheson. "Maude, the maid girl to the ladies, says there is some mess left lying outside Miss Kitty's door. It seems it is below Maude to deal with it herself."

Truth be told, I do not wish to step further into the house. I do not wish to come across the new Laird, who cared not one jot for the old Laird. I do not wish to see any of the ladies, who chose not to attend the funeral just because of the weather, fearing their pretty dresses might be spoiled.

I just want to rush outside, take Father's arm and go home.

But Mistress Matheson and Ishbel look worn to the bones with work and grief, and so of course I do as I am bid. Hoping the dog is safe shut in the drawing room with its master, I quickly pad up the dark back stairs and find myself once again on the landing of the floor above.

In a blink, I have hurried past the Black Crow's room, past more doors to unseen rooms, past a grand staircase with thick polished bannister – the stairs for the rich folk, of course – and am headed towards the far end of the corridor. There, a large window spills light on to a mound of something by a closed door.

Coming close, I see the mound is a white pillow, though it is clearly stained. And beside it, a broken cup that must have contained tea or coffee.

Just as I bend to take it, wondering how this mishap might have happened, a shrill screech of fury and a smashing sound makes me leap away from the door.

"Shh! My darling, quiet yourself!" says a voice inside.

"How can I, Mama!" I hear Miss Kitty say sharply. "I tell you, I will *not* stay here. We *must* go back to London. Just because we now own this drab island, it doesn't mean it must be our home!"

"My sweet," Mrs Palmer-Reeves tries to console her. "Your father just explained it to you. We dared not tell you of his money worries before, but now, inheriting this place solves our problems. We can rent out the London house, and live here for a year or two quite comfortably. And by then, Papa's business interests will be fully recovered, I'm sure, and—"

"But if we had money worries, why did Papa take in that stupid woman in the first place?"

There is a creak on the wooden treads behind me, and the sound of a little gasp. I hardly dare turn round, and yet I do – and see the Black Crow standing at the top of the grand staircase, a gloved hand to her lace veil.

She has heard the loud, harshly spoken words, it seems,

and has recognised herself in the mean description just given.

Still, it is not my place to be here, or to be seen to be eavesdropping. And so with trembling hands, I grab the pillow and broken teacup and scurry past the statue-still old lady with a muttered, "Pardon me", as I head towards the servants' staircase.

"Oh, what a waste of a bonnie cup!" sighs Mistress Matheson as I hurtle downstairs and into the haven of the kitchen and drop my burden on the wooden table.

"Here … for your trouble," says Ishbel, handing me a thick slice of ham from a leg she is carving.

But I have no taste for it. Instead, I shake my head, throw my thick shawl over me and slip out of the back door.

Father studies me as I walk towards him and the other good men that stand with him. His soaked red hair and beard are darkened to a deep rust.

"Away home with you now, Bridie," he says softly. "It is not a day to be out if you can help it."

Staring up at his strong face, I feel my own rage returning, that a man like he and the other elders might be ignored in such a callous way.

"Father, it is not fair!" I announce.

"Aye, but it is what it is, my dear," he says calmly.

Something about him using Mother's words makes my anger rise … but *this* time it is directed towards Father and Mr Matheson and Mr Beaton and the others. They are strong-minded, true-hearted men; why do they not stand up to a feeble character like Mr Palmer-Reeves?

"Because it is the way of the Highlands," I practically hear Mother patiently telling me, telling us *all* as we grew up. "Forever, folk lived in clans, with a chieftain to watch over them, like a father to his family. And Mr Menzies might be a laird in a suit and not a great chieftain with a kilt and sword, but he treats us well, does he not?"

Not every father is kind, though; and just as some chieftains of the distant past must have been bullies and rogues, we know from the nearer past of the Highlands that plenty of lairds have treated their folk more like beasts of the fields than humans.

And we may well have one of *that* type about to rule over us now, which makes me want to fly off from Tornish even more, and get every islander to rise like a flock and leave with me!

But we are flightless, stuck, trapped.

CHAPTER 6

When she has clouded thoughts, who else should a girl confide in, if not her mother?

"I am trying to be like you and be accepting of the way things are ... but it is hard," I say, as I set the posy of wild flowers by Mother's small headstone. "And I am not the only one struggling. Effie - she is worse than ever! She is seeing signs in every overcast sky, every burnt oatcake, every hen that does not lay. She is certain that bad times are ahead, and because of it her temper ... oh, her temper is high indeed!"

Father has tried to calm my sister but she will not settle. Though I know he too worries what the future may hold. It has been near a month since Mr Menzies' funeral, and yet Mr Palmer-Reeves chooses not to become familiar with his tenants. He has been back and forth to the mainland, seeing to legal matters, Father presumes. And this week past the whole family were gone to Glasgow, where Mrs Palmer-Reeves and Miss Kitty planned to buy some "better" things for the house, she announced to Mistress Matheson before they left.

In the new Laird's absence, across the island, the mood is very brooding, as they worry what his plans will be for the place. And now that Mr Simpson has packed away his hateful cane and taken his leave of the school, the islanders know not when the next teacher will arrive for the benefit of their children, as the new Laird must organise that with the school authorities. But is that something he would bother himself to do? He certainly didn't bother to see Father and the other elders that afternoon in the rain, after the funeral.

Yet undaunted, Father has promised the people of the townships that he and the other elders will ask for a meeting with Mr Palmer-Reeves as soon as is possible. But until then, the only thing certain is that this afternoon, a boat is expected, bringing Mr Palmer-Reeves and his family and their "better things" to us, for good or for ill.

"And Ishbel, well, she is so very quiet that I wish she would shout and scold me so that I recognise my own sister," I carry on to Mother. "Of course, she is worrying that the new Laird may wish to dispense with the workers at the Big House and replace them with his own people, brought from his London residence."

Wouldn't it be a wonder if Mother could answer me back? How I would love her advice, to give to my sisters. Not that either of them would heed me, of course.

I close my eyes and try to see her face, to imagine her telling me gently that it is what it is, but her face is hazy to me, softened with the mists of time. Why, I'm even seeing the softening of Mr Menzies' features in my head, and he has only been departed for a few short weeks.

But I think that if – by some mystic, magic force – Mother's words suddenly *did* come to me, I would simply hear her fretting that her three daughters are not the sisterly friends they once were. She oftentimes said that women bear their hardships in a quieter way than men, and felt most strongly that *all* young girls should learn to look out for one another. Of course, with Mother's passing, Ishbel and Effie unfortunately took Mother's wisdom to mean they must look after me by bossing and scolding and—

"Little Bird!" a shout rings out.

I glance up – past the white stone urn perched on the headstone that marks Mr Menzies' resting place – and see Will sprinting down the lane that passes the churchyard, his cap in his hand lest it flies off his head in his haste.

Quickly, I kiss my fingertips and press them against Mother's modest headstone and push myself upright. It's a moment's work – though not perhaps a very respectful one – to fling my legs over the low wall in a flurry of skirts.

"What is it?" I ask my friend, whose cheeks burn red

from the effort of running. He leans on the dyke I have just leapt over to catch his breath.

"The boat is here," he pants, leaning his hands on his britches as he gasps. "The new Laird has told me … he has told me to fetch some men to help unload his goods and baggage. A ferry has come too, carrying horses and two gigs that are being taken off."

No sooner has Will panted those words aloud than a dull, thunderous clatter of hooves comes thundering along the lane from the direction of the harbour.

At the sound of it, I find my weakened hand flailing for a grip of something, anything, to keep me balanced, for the world seems momentarily unsteady to me.

And what my fingers fix on is a sprawling branch of the yew tree whose leaves in the summer shelter Mother's grave.

"Hey, boy!" shouts the moustachioed gentleman, pulling his horse to a standstill as he towers over my friend. "Did I not give you specific instructions to fetch some assistance?"

At the same time Mr Palmer-Reeves barks his orders, a fine little gig trundles along to join him, pulled by a white horse and with the little cairn terrier trotting alongside. Behind the driver of the gig sit Mrs Palmer-Reeves and Miss Kitty. For now, her eyes once again dart over me, settling on my foot that shows beneath my skirts, and the odd angle of it. Her mouth makes a shape that shows her disgust better than words ever could.

For a hot, angry moment, I think to step back, so that the trunk of the yew tree blocks the girl's view of me, but I have never been shamed of anything about myself, so instead I put my twisted foot forward and lift my chin high.

Miss Kitty meets my eye, then looks away, as if the very sight of me is displeasing to her. So it seems all the "better things" she and her mother have bought have not improved her mood any.

"Don't waste your breath on the boy, dear," the new mistress calls out to her husband in the meantime. "Remember, he will only have the most basic of English."

As Will and I listen, understanding every word spoken, I find that I am now staring at the most peculiar thing balanced above the mistress's head. Held by a stick, it is a tiny confection of lace in the shape of a very small dome. It is like a fool's version of the black umbrella Mr Menzies uses – I should say *used* – to keep the rain from him when he paid visits to his tenants. But there is no rain on this glorious early June day…

"Shoo! Off with you! GET MEN!" the mistress yelps at Will, waggling a white-gloved hand at him.

Will frowns at her, as if he has no knowledge at all of her meaning – which makes me shake with laughter that I must not let loose.

"MEN!" Mr Palmer-Reeves repeats, pointing in the vague direction of the lane up ahead, where a fork leads left to the Big House and right towards the nearby crofts, and onwards to the rest of the island. "GET MEN TO THE HARBOUR. NOW!"

His last words are near lost as a second, less fine gig catches up to the first, this one containing the Black Crow and the sulky maid I saw her with on the Palmer-Reeves' last visit. The Black Crow's head inclines towards me … is she looking at me too? What thoughts are writ on the face beneath the veil, I wonder? What I *do* know is that I should think of her now as Miss Tulliver. "Miss" and not "Mrs", Ishbel assured me. So perhaps the old lady is a spinster great-aunt, and not grandmother? Ishbel's job is to help cook and clean and carry below-stairs, so she can help me no more with that notion.

With a sigh and a sharp shake of his head, Mr Palmer-Reeves impatiently pushes his horse forward into a gallop, and the two gigs quickly start up and follow him off along the lane.

Before they disappear from view, it pleases me to see the dainty carriages hit the rutted dry mud up ahead, shaking the very bones of the travellers inside.

"MEN! GET MEN TO THE HARBOUR NOW!" barks Will, sticking his chest out and mimicking our new Laird.

With a grin, I snap a long twig off the overhanging

tree and hold it upright above me, as if I too had one of those lacy fool's umbrellas.

"Shoo! Off with you!" I similarly mimic the new mistress.

Will and I are both lost in laughter when we hear an almighty clatter.

"Confound it!" someone exclaims.

And there, in the lane, is a young gentleman, wearing some manner of floppy cravat at his neck, and with a maroon-coloured coat that is made of the loveliest of soft cloth, the like of which I have never seen. He has about him a bag strapped to his back, another worn across his chest, his hands free to carry wooden boxes by their leather handles. There is a contraption of wood – long strips fixed together somehow – on the dusty ground, which he must have been conveying over his shoulder or had tucked under one arm.

"Here," Will says in English, trying to pick the thing up since the young gentleman would struggle to do so, he is so burdened.

I hurry to help too: as Will lifts the long strips they splay out in a most peculiar way, and he is unable to contain them.

"Thank you," says the young gentleman, laying his boxes to the ground and wrestling with the errant legs of the wooden contraption.

"What is this?" I ask him outright, first in Gaelic and

then quickly in English.

"It's an easel," says the young man, spinning the thing upside down and then setting it upright. Now we can see that the three strips are legs, and that at about the height of the young man's waist there is some kind of ledge.

He looks at myself and Will and sees that we are none the wiser.

"I am an artist. When I paint, I place my canvas here. Do you see?" he says, tapping at the ledge that lies halfway up the long strips.

"An artist, you say?" I repeat, now seeing that his dress and long, floppy hair are different indeed from the starched-suited gentlemen that have come to the island in the past to visit Mr Menzies.

"I am indeed. But I should introduce myself… How do you do? My name is Samuel Mitford," he says politely, as if Will and I were a well-dressed, well-mannered lord and lady of the manor instead of two barefoot and bamboozled children. "Pleased to make your acquaintance."

"H … hello," I reply haltingly, as I shyly shake his solid hand with my weak one. If he notices, he says nothing. "I'm Little Bird. Bridie MacKerrie, that is."

"Little Bird?" says this Mr Samuel Mitford, with an interested raise of his eyebrows. "How poetic."

The foolish rush of heat to my cheeks is not poetic.

But I am very, very grateful and surprised by the compliment. I am also relieved that his attention is now turned to Will so he cannot see my giddiness at his words.

"And I am William Beaton," says Will assuredly. "And I must go, since I am on an urgent errand for the new Laird!"

With that, he rushes off, taking the right turn where the lane forks, so that he can find the men at work on the land nearby my township.

"Well, I am quite lost," says the young gentleman, looking this way and that. "Might you show me the way to go, Little Bird?"

How strange it is to hear someone who is neither Will nor dear Mr Menzies call me that name! But strange in a pleasing way, I must confess.

I drop a quick curtsey, then pick up one of the boxes that are laid on the ground.

"The Big House is this way," I tell him, heading for the left turn of the fork in the lane. "Are you kin of the new Laird, sir, if I may ask?"

"You certainly may, and no, I am not," says Mr Mitford with a smile, as he picks up his easel contraption with a rattle and a clank and follows me. "I am tasked to paint a portrait of Mr Palmer-Reeves, here on his estate, and it was arranged that I meet him and his family in Glasgow just this morning, before we set sail."

"Oh. Will you be staying long on Tornish?" I ask, knowing nothing of how long a thing such as a portrait might take.

"A few weeks," he replies. "My … what a view!"

As he exclaims at the sight of the Big House towering above the strong walls that Father built, with the woods like a great, green blanket behind it, I can't help but frown.

"Sir, that is no view. You must climb the Glas Crags to see a true view. Or visit the waterfall, or the standing stones on the moor, or the lochan, or the pretty cove to the north…"

My babbled words are drowned out by a frantic barking from the little cairn terrier, tearing out of the open ironwork gates towards us as if we needed a fanfare for our arrival.

"Ha! This little fellow was quite taken with the seagulls that accompanied us on our trip today. He was barking his hellos at them on the deck of the steamer!" says Mr Mitford, while Patch bounces and darts around our feet as we enter the courtyard. "Though it earned him a smack or two from his master…"

Of course, I have already seen how at ease Mr Palmer-Reeves is with his stick around the dog. I am troubled at the memory, yet for now my mind is fixed on the steamer and the adventure it must be to sail on such a thing.

"How I'd love to see the rooms of a ship like that," I say wistfully, as we walk closer to the front entrance of the Big House, with the heavy double doors open wide to the tiled hall beyond. "I have not even been on the little ferry boat that comes to us from the mainland."

"Well, perhaps while I am here on Tornish, I can describe it to you," says my companion, "and tell you tales of Glasgow and the like!"

"Oh, thank you, Mr Mitford!" I say, a small ripple of pleasure in my stomach at the very thought.

"Samuel, please," he replies, as we walk though the tall entrance gates and into the grounds. "I tell you what – in return, Little Bird, perhaps one day you can be my guide, and show me these truly special views Tornish has to offer? I would very much like to see and sketch the landscape while I am here."

"Samuel"? I cannot call a grown man, a gentleman, by his first name, surely! Though now that I study his friendly face, I see he cannot be very much older than Will's brother, or the Matheson lads. Past his twentieth year, I'd guess, but no more than twenty-two or three.

"Yes, I would like that, Mr— Mr Samuel," I say with a nod, while he shrugs and laughs kindly at my shyness.

At the sound of his laugh, something catches my eye … a movement in the darkness of the hall of the house up ahead. I blink my eyes and see the Black Crow – Miss Tulliver – standing at the bottom of the huge staircase. She must have been observing us, and now that she has been caught, the woman in the shadows turns and disappears upstairs.

How the old lady puzzles me; I never thought how unknowable a person is if their face is covered. You cannot be sure whether you must fear them or pity them, whether they watch you with curiosity or with loathing…

"Bridie!" I hear my name urgently hissed, and see my sister Ishbel hurrying over to me, one hand gathering up her skirts and apron as she runs, the other holding a bat of bent cane-work I know to be a carpet-beater. I hope she does not mean to chase me from the courtyard with it!

But the joking thought flits away as I see the stark warning in Ishbel's grey eyes. And in that moment, I realise my place is not at the *front* of the Big House, certainly not now Mr Menzies is gone.

"I'm sorry, my sister is in need of me," I tell Mr Samuel, as I put down his boxes and go to meet Ishbel halfway.

"Thank you for your help, Little Bird!" Mr Samuel calls out, as he watches Ishbel press her hand against the small of my back and turn me around towards the big iron gates.

"Quick," she whispers, though there is no one close by to hear. "You must not let the new folk see you, or we will both be in trouble."

"But I was only helping the Laird's guest," I protest, practically being rushed off my feet by my sister's haste. "He is an artist, come to paint Mr—"

"Well and good," Ishbel interrupts, "but you are not a child, Bridie. You *know* we must all be careful, till we get a measure of Mr Palmer-Reeves."

For the first time in a long while I take a proper look at my eldest sister. Her face – as thin and pale as Effie's is round and fair – seems gaunt and haunted. Sallow circles lie beneath her black-lashed eyes as if all the weight of the world rests on her shoulders.

And with reason, I suppose. Ishbel wants nothing to change. She wants her work here at the Big House to continue till such time as she marries Donal Matheson (though she would shush me for saying that, as she is but seventeen, of course, and so nothing is set or certain). She pictures herself in a cosy house not far from Father's, where she can bring up any children that she and her future husband are blessed with. She wants all this, but Mr Palmer-Reeves – without knowing – has the power to take that away from her…

"Before you go, have this," says Ishbel, pulling a lump of fresh bread from the pocket of her apron and pressing it into my good hand. "Mistress Matheson gave me it for my dinner. Now, get yourself home; Effie will have chores for you to do, I am sure of it."

LITTLE BIRD FLIES

I am sure of it too. And now I find myself shooed to the far side of the gates, as Ishbel retreats back inside the tall perimeter wall with a wan smile.

Turning to walk off along the rutted lane, I look down at the food Ishbel has given me. The bread must be made from wheat that the old Laird had stocked; it is much lighter and finer than the bannocks of oat that we have at home.

Before I know it, and before I take the first bite, I am skipping like a little child with gladness, but glad for what I am not really sure.

For this treat of crusty bread?

No; it is for what my secret, guilty self *feels* this very moment.

While the whole island waits and worries and watches the incomers with dread – my father and sisters included – I am suddenly shot through with the sense of hope and happiness. Because at last, something has *happened* on this tiny island. Even though I miss Mr Menzies with all my heart, even with the look of that haughty Miss Kitty and the ignorance of her so-called educated father, it feels as if … as if today, this afternoon, a window might have opened to the world!

For there has never been a person such as Mr Samuel visit Tornish. A gentleman who talks to me and Will as if we are worth talking to. And an artist, no less, with his colours and imagination and stories, I hope. I *so* wish to speak with him and hear what a city as great as Glasgow is like. Is it full of long roads filled with the likes of the Big House, as far as the eye can see? And I hear there are buildings laid out on land the size of fields where hundreds of people work, making iron or cloth that it is supplied the whole country over; nay the *world* over. I've heard Father say there's a harbour full of steamships and sail ships and hustle and bustle. What does a city like that look like and sound like? *Those* are the stories I want to hear…

As I muse on this, eating and skipping my way home, the sun slips away, casting a cold shadow where there was warmth.

Gazing up at the bruise-coloured clouds above, wet drops dot my bare arms. If I was Effie, I might think the elements were warning me not to be so foolish or fanciful. But I quickly shake the thought away, for I am not my sister, looking for reckonings of trouble at every turn.

A stormy sky is just a stormy sky.

It is what it is, and I look forward to whatever small pleasures the future will bring.

Some change can be good, can it not?

A sudden crack of thunder sends me scurrying quickly for home and shelter, lest the hammering rain wash the desperate hope inside me clean away.

CHAPTER 7

I hate Sundays.

There: another secret my mother would be shocked and shamed by if she knew of it.

But it is true; this day of the week fills me with dread. The preacher that comes over on the ferry from the mainland is very old. So old he is deaf, and thinks his mumblings in the church are adequate for us to hear his supposed wise words. They are not.

And I do not hate Sundays only because of the deaf preacher and his droned sermons that no one can fathom … it is because I must wear my best clothes, which includes black wool stockings that itch till I could scream and ill-fitting black boots that were first Ishbel's, then Effie's. To be truthful, no boot, no matter how keenly crafted, would neatly match my twisted foot. It is trapped now, and even with laces loosely fastened, the bones and muscles protest at the tight grip of this leather restraint.

"Bridie! Be still!" Ishbel snaps at me as we stand

outside the church with all the other tenant folk of Tornish.

Like them, our family is waiting to thank the preacher for today's mumbled wisdom – though he might merely have reeled off every meal he has eaten over the last month, for all we understood of his sermon. But the new Laird and his household are first to speak with the preacher, of course.

"Leave me be, I am disturbing no one!" I tell Ishbel, as I put my boot against the wall of the church so that I can reach my lace and try to slacken it further. Though that is not so easy; my bad hand is good enough for most that I need it to do, but the very smallness of the knot is vexing to my weakened fingers.

"For shame!" hisses Ishbel. "Folk can see your petticoat!"

"And folk can see *yours*, hanging on the line every wash day," I mutter back, under my breath, as I work hard at the stubborn knot.

At this angle, if I tilt my head a little, I can also slyly glance the way of the Laird and those who straggle around him. Apart from the few London servants that have newly joined the household, the Mistress is there, as you would expect, holding her tiny fool's umbrella above her head, to the amusement of the island children. Miss Kitty is causing amazement and giggles in equal measure with her enormous new bonnet, made of neatly woven straw with a fluff of feathers stuck upon it. And close by, in her shroud of dark wool, silk and lace is the Black Crow, Miss Tulliver, who seems to shrink into herself as much as Miss Kitty stands haughty and proud.

It has been more than a week since the new Laird came back from his jaunt to Glasgow, and until today, no one had seen hide nor hair of him or his family except for those, like Ishbel and Mistress Matheson, who work in the Big House. Though Ishbel, whose time is spent mostly in the kitchens and outhouses, has in truth seen little of the family, except for Miss Tulliver taking solitary walks around the walled garden. Ishbel also talks of the little dog, who on occasion scampers where he should not and gets a smack for it, and the steward, ladies' maids and grooms and such from London who all have nothing but contempt for the islander staff who wait on them.

"Here," Ishbel says with a weary sigh. "Give me your foot, Bridie, and I'll try to ease it."

At her for-once-kindly order, I hop around so that my back now leans against the hard, cool stone of the wall, and let my sister take my ankle in her hand.

"I can manage, you know," I tell her, though I am glad of her help. "You could go and be with your friends…"

I mean that she can be with Donal Matheson, but I dare not say so for the glower I would get.

"Oh, I am not much enjoying their talk just now,"

Ishbel says, also struggling with the reluctant fastening. She does not see that Donal has already stepped away from his own brother Fergus and Will's brother George and the other lads and has walked over to seek her out. And she has not realised that he has heard her last remark.

"I can't say we are much 'enjoying' our talk either, Ishbel," he says, a dark look clouding his face. "But these things need to be said, do they not?"

With no proper sightings of Mr Palmer-Reeves, the island folks' thoughts have begun to turn troubled – especially those of the young men, like Donal, Fergus and George.

"But what purpose does it serve to fear the worst?" Ishbel chides him. "We all may do well enough when the new Laird is quite settled. And once Father has a chance to talk with him, I am sure he can put folks' minds at rest."

"And when will that be, eh, Ishbel?" Donal demands, losing patience with his beloved for the first time ever, I am sure. "Mr Palmer-Reeves has not set a date for an audience with the elders. And when, *if*, he ever does, what happens should he announce that every one of us is to be driven away, and fine flocks of Cheviot sheep take our place?"

At that I have a sudden memory of Mr Palmer-Reeves and his lawyer friend, examining the paintings

in the great hall of the Big House, when first they came
to Tornish.

"But that will not happen – the new master does not
like sheep!" I blurt out, hoping that foolish-sounding
snatch of remembered conversation would help reassure
Donal and the others.

But Donal pays me no mind; his passions are high and
he is already impatiently turning back to his friends.

"Ach, Donal supposes we all must think as he does, or
we are fools!" Ishbel mutters, without realising I would
describe her in the very same way.

She stares after him, but I am staring at who is coming
towards us. Effie's frowning glare is firmly fixed on me.

"Bridie!" she calls out.

What now – is she about to scold me for having too
much knitted stocking on show or the like?

"Is it paining you?" she asks as she reaches us, and lays
a warm hand on my raised ankle.

I am lost for words for a moment, as I am in those rare
moments that Effie or Ishbel soften towards me. Even
in the cramped box bed we share, I am at the mercy of
their digging elbows and thudding knees as they harshly
claim the space in their sleep, with me in the middle,
inching in my turns lest I disturb them.

But before I manage to form my words into an
answer, Effie turns to Ishbel. "We must ask Father to
buy her new boots. Softer ones."

"Yes," Ishbel agrees. "We'll ask him later if—"

"No, no!" I say quickly.

I understand, as my sisters do, that Father has money set aside. Money he has earned down the years from the good stone-work he has done on Tornish and on the mainland too, as news of his skills spreads. He keeps this treasure trove of coins and notes in a prettily decorated tin box that was once Mother's. It is tucked away in the eaves somewhere, and there it must stay till Father decides that the time is right to spend it. Ishbel says Mother once told her the purpose of it, and it is for us. For Ishbel and Effie, for me and for Lachlan. It is money to help us when we marry, to buy us things for the homes that we girls will have with our husbands and Lachlan will have with his wife.

Something curdles in the pit of my stomach at the thought of that money and its purpose. The idea of my own husband and my own croft here on the island, and my own kettles and pots and beds and chickens makes me want to do one thing and one thing only: grab my foot away from Ishbel and run, run, run for the Glas Crags and the view and the sea and the sky and the clouds.

Where I can fill my tight lungs with clean, sharp air.

Where my eyes can seek the horizon; oh, that faraway horizon to the west and America and freedom…

But the truth – in the here and now – is that I

cannot seem like an ungrateful daughter who would reject such a loving gift. So the next best that I can do is reject new boots, which would take away from the money that my sisters and brother deserve more than me.

"I will get some fat, and work it in the leather," I say keenly. "That will ease it, I'm sure."

"I'm not sure that will be enough," Ishbel says kindly but firmly. "I think Effie is right and—"

"Ha! Is this some strange Highland Fling?" comes a voice that I instantly know, with a rush in my chest, to be Mr Samuel's.

I ignore the flutterings of shyness; I have had no sightings of the artist since he arrived and I am more than pleased to make his acquaintance again.

My sisters immediately curtsey, but I cannot, since Ishbel still has my foot in her hand.

Instead I hop a little to keep my balance and say, "It is indeed. Would you like me to teach it to you?"

Ishbel and Effie gasp at my cheek – and Mr Samuel smiles even more brightly. Till he shocks my sisters by putting his hand out to greet them.

"You are Ishbel; I remember you from the first day I arrived at the house," he says with a courteous nod of the head, before turning to Effie. "And you are so very alike, and must be another sister to Little Bird?"

Mr Samuel's belief that we have some similarity

makes the three of us turn to each other and laugh; it is such a fanciful notion! What we have in common is a shared feeling that we are so very different from each other, and not just in looks… Ishbel, serious and grown beyond her years; Effie, bossy and superstitious, and I … what am I? Small but irksome to my sisters, and full of secrets in my own eyes.

"This is Effie," I say, taking the trouble to name our middle sister, since she is too affronted to talk in front of this stranger.

"Pleased to meet you," Mr Samuel says with a bow, and in this moment I see that he is not too much older than Fergus and Donal Matheson, who are both a little past their twenty-first year, I think. "Now, Little Bird, I have been very busy painting your Laird in his study. But he wishes the background to be some scenic panorama of the island that I must find and paint *without* him, as he has much business to attend to. Would you fulfil your promise and show me some splendid vistas? Tomorrow, perhaps?"

My sisters look lost for words and slightly scandalised. But of course I will say yes. Having no school at the moment, Will and Lachlan can come with me, so Father will not mind.

I am about to ask when Mr Samuel would like to set off, when we are joined by three unsmiling ladies. Though the third, I suppose, *might* be smiling, but I would not know of it because of the veil she wears.

As soon as Ishbel becomes aware of their presence, she lets my foot fall to the ground, and we MacKerrie sisters do our best, most polite bob to the new Laird's wife, daughter and Miss Tulliver, hidden in her wraps of lace and mourning.

Well, perhaps it might be expected that Mrs Palmer-Reeves would engage us in some pleasantries, but it seems she has no taste for that.

"I hear you work at the house," she says directly to Ishbel, in a manner that has no warmth. "Do you understand me? I expect you would have some English, thanks to Mr Menzies."

"Yes, ma'am," Ishbel replies politely.

"Good. Well, Miss Kitty has alerted me to your hair," Mistress Palmer-Reeves continues in a stiff, dry tone. "And now I can see she is correct in what she has told me; the style of it is very fanciful for one of your standing. I would expect it to be of a plainer nature when you work for us."

"Yes, ma'am," Ishbel answers in a voice now no louder than a whisper. A blush of red flushes on my sister's pale, hollowed cheeks.

A blush of red flushes on my own cheeks. Why should these women belittle my sister so? What is it to them if she likes to braid and coil her hair, as long as she cleans and scrubs their chamberpots well?

Oh, I see that my face must be showing my flare of anger; Miss Kitty stares at me so, as if she would very much like to reach across and slap me with the soft, white kid gloves she is holding in her hand.

"So is Mr Palmer-Reeves quite determined on a walk this afternoon?" Mr Samuel says suddenly, in a most agreeable tone, as if he is trying to pour balm on this painful exchange.

"Yes, yes … as long as the weather holds in this blessed place!" says the Mistress, glaring up at the sky as if she wishes it ill for not behaving.

And now I am relieved to see her move off, with a heavy shuffle of her puffed skirts, Miss Kitty following with her own shuffle and rustle, and a look of disdain for us as she goes. The silent Miss Tulliver attempts to join them, but – thanks to the veil that must hamper her sight – she stumbles, and both Mr Samuel and myself are the first to reach her, each of us grabbing an elbow to steady the old lady.

And with that steadying grab, on my side I notice the soft cloth of the Black Crow's sleeve ride up, making a gap between cuff and glove. I cannot help stare at the skin on her wrist; it is very wrinkled, as you might expect of one of advanced years. But the wrinkles are puckered in an unusual way, and are a very dark pink. It reminds me of something I have seen, or perhaps been told…?

And then I hear words spoken in a way I did not expect.

"Thank you," says a quiet, uncertain voice from beneath the veil. "You are very kind."

And that voice confounds me … for it is – I am suddenly very sure – a *young person's* voice.

Wait… I have been mistaken all this time? A quick glance at Ishbel shows that she is equally surprised to know that this lady living under the roof of the Big House is not who either of us supposed her to be.

I quickly turn back to stare at the Black Crow – at Miss Tulliver, I mean – with new eyes, but her head is bowed, as if she stares down at her feet to remind them where they need to be placed.

What of Mr Samuel … having met the family in Glasgow and stayed with them this last week, did he already know what we have only just discovered? The expression on his face is not one of surprise, certainly, so I must guess he *is* aware that he is in the company of a young lady. But what his expression does convey is something I saw just now in my sisters' eyes as they fussed over me: tenderness and concern.

My secret self shivers a little at the thought of tomorrow, when I might see Mr Samuel again.

For I will keep my promise and reveal to him the special places of the island – and perhaps he may reveal to me what he knows of the Black Crow…?

CHAPTER 8

Tomorrow is still not here.

Yet I am once again – unexpectedly – in the company of Mr Samuel.

Sadly, it is not *only* Mr Samuel.

For Mistress Palmer-Reeves, Miss Kitty and Miss Tulliver are in our kitchen, in our home.

Outside, the new Laird is getting Father to show him the byre, the field, the cattle in the sweet green pastures.

Inside, the ladies – accompanied by Mr Samuel – wish to take tea, after their tiring afternoon stroll, it seems. The group arrived a few minutes ago with this *order*, rather than request. How lucky it was not any earlier; we girls have only just taken a turn each with the tin bath, washing ourselves and our hair in front of the fire. But it is bad enough; we are in our oldest work clothes, with our good stuff set away again in the chests. Our hair is loose and damp down to our waists, and certainly not tidy, as it should be. And I know the visitors will have seen our petticoats and drawers fluttering on the washing line nearby (for shame).

Confused, poorly dressed, with hair wild as banshees, Effie and I hover either side of the fireplace, not knowing quite what to do with ourselves. Ishbel, at least, has the role of host to keep her busy. She is perched on the stool in front of the fire.

"The water will boil shortly," she says, settling the big black kettle on the grate, now that she has stoked up the fire. "Won't you take a seat?"

She asks this because Mistress Palmer-Reeves and Miss Kitty are walking about the room, examining our things with a look of curious disdain. The plates on our dresser, the wooden bowls and tin cups and horn spoons laid neatly on the table, the candlesticks and china dog ornaments and clock on the mantle above the fire ... they may not be as expensive and special as the painted porcelain and polished silver *they* are used to, but our things are clean and good and precious to us.

"Sit!" Mistress Palmer-Reeves says smartly to Miss Tulliver, as if she were the little dog that Lachlan is playing with in the yard just now.

The Black Crow perches quickly on the long, wooden settle, with a lightness and speed that shows that she is indeed a younger lady, and not some stiffened elderly woman, as I'd supposed her to be. Mr Samuel immediately sits beside her, an open book of some kind in his lap.

It is most peculiar to see them both there, as this bench is where Lachlan and I sit of an evening, while Father and Ishbel and Effie take the three good chairs.

"Are there cattle through there?" Miss Kitty asks, pointing to the rooms beyond this one, her nostrils quivering as if she can already smell their dung.

A rattle crosses my chest at her words. Yes, there are still a few ancient blackhouses and cottages across the island where folk – old folk mostly – live in this time-honoured way, with one half of their building made cosy and homely for themselves, while the other room is a safe, dry shelter for their animals. But so many of the crofters have better houses now. And Father built us the best on Tornish after Lachlan was born. We have three rooms; this fine one we are in now, to cook in and sit in and talk and read and hear Father play his whistle of an evening while we sing along. The other big room is where myself and my sisters sleep in the box bed, with its doors that we can close when the winter winds do their best to chill the walls of our sturdy house. And in between the two big rooms, there is the small one that Father and Lachlan share.

"We have a byre outside for the livestock," Ishbel tells Miss Kitty plainly, talking of the old cottage in the yard, that was the home all we children were born in.

She says no more than that, but I see Miss Kitty peering, as if she wishes to be shown what rooms *are* next door. With all my heart I do not wish this yellow-haired poppet to look with her mean, pitying gaze on the places where my sisters and I lay our heads and dream our different dreams...

It seems Effie feels the same.

"Will you not sit? Here, these will make you more comfortable..."

As quick as a darting sparrow my sister takes some of the cushions from the settle and places them on the wooden chairs, then hurries to her spot by the mantle once again.

Mistress Palmer-Reeves checks the cushions to see if they are to her liking, or to check if they are *clean* enough for her liking, and finally deigns to sit down. Her daughter follows suit, I am relieved to see.

"So where is your mother?" Mistress Palmer-Reeves asks bluntly, as if she thinks Mother wanting indeed not to be here to greet her.

The rumbling in my chest becomes painful.

If folk here speak of our mother, it is with softness in their voices and fond memory in their hearts – especially the womenfolk, young and old, who loved her dearly for her kindness and friendship towards them. And I want it no other way.

"She died some years ago, ma'am," says Ishbel, trying to tie her hair into some kind of braid, though wet tendrils still spill about her shoulders like black seaweed.

At that, myriad thoughts connect in my mind, like links in a chain. I see the churchyard where Mother lies, alongside two little brothers and a sister who lived only days each before they were gone. But one little sister, Mairi, may have been hale and hearty and still the eldest sister to us all if she had not met with a terrible accident. This firstborn of the family had just learned to walk, but not yet learned to heed danger, and so tumbled into the fire, where her little clothes caught alight.

No one in our family ever talks of it. But I have heard of that wretched time... Will's own mother told him and he told me; the awful pain that poor Mairi suffered. The hope felt by our parents, when, after a few months, she seemed better, healed − though she carried pink wrinkles of the burns on her arms and chest as unhappy mementoes. The sadness when winter came and her lungs were too hurt from the smoke of the fire for her to stand the illness that finally struck her down.

And there − that scrap of thought; the pink wrinkles of Mairi's burns.

I sensed some familiarity when I saw Miss Tulliver's wrist outside church earlier today.

So she has suffered in a similar way?

With a wrench of pity, I risk a glance over at the settle − and see that Miss Tulliver's head is down, and her shoulders are heaving. Mr Samuel sees it too, and − quickly shoving his book in his coat pocket − puts an arm around her.

"Are you unwell, Miss Tulliver?" he asks.

"Caroline!" barks the Mistress. "Sit up straight! Compose yourself!"

I cannot stand still and hear the Black Crow be spoken to as if she is an annoyance, when she is clearly in some distress.

"Will you come outside for a moment?" I ask, my bare feet crossing the flagstones before I get to the door and open it wide; wide to the rolling hills, the blue sky that meets them – not to mention our washed, white underthings doing their whirling dance. "There is a seat out there and you can get some air…"

I half expect the Black Crow to shake her head and stay where she is. But no: almost shielded by Mr Samuel she hurries outdoors before she is told she cannot.

"Please, this way," I say, ushering Miss Tulliver over towards the byre.

Miss Tulliver glides quickly over to it, as if she has set eyes on an oasis in the desert, instead of a humble stool where I sang my songs and filled the pail with the cows' good milk this morning.

"Can I fetch you anything?" Mr Samuel asks her as she sits down.

"No, no…" Miss Tulliver replies, her voice catching in her throat, the way it does when tears have a hold of you. "I am sorry, I was taken aback by the mention of your mother's loss. My own died last year."

The Black Crow is looking up at me, and through the lace of her veil, I make out eyes wide and searching. I suddenly feel so very sure that Miss Tulliver is deeply, frighteningly lonely, locked in her mourning prison.

"I'm sorry to hear that," I say politely, matching her gaze instead of lowering it as I ought to.

"Thank you," Miss Tulliver replies a little unsteadily. "May I ask what she died of?"

"The wasting," I say in Gaelic, since I do not know its name in English.

"Tuberculosis?" says Mr Samuel, recognising my meaning from the way I clutch my chest. I nod, and try to push the picture of my mother in her last coughing, choking days from my mind.

So there is *my* answer. Of course, it would not be polite for me to ask the same question of Miss Tulliver. I know I should be meek in the company of my betters; Mother would tell me so very surely.

But I also know that I cannot stop my runaway mouth sometimes.

"What happened to *your* mother?" I ask her, too boldly, I know.

"There was a fire, in our house." Miss Tulliver is kind enough to answer me honestly, and without rancour at my cheek. "Mr Palmer-Reeves is my guardian, so I came to live with his family after that."

LITTLE BIRD FLIES

Ah. Those few short words make me understand Miss Tulliver's situation very clear. As she is so obviously a fine lady, I imagine her house must have been large. Now, if a candle is left unattended or an oil lamp tipped over in a little cottage such as ours, it can quickly be doused or the tenants swiftly flee. But in a large place, I imagine, a fire could rage and roar with abandon, trapping those inside in faraway rooms. A mother could die. A daughter could be injured.

But I do not understand what Miss Tulliver says or does next.

Reaching out to me, she gently takes hold of my weak hand in hers.

"I envy you," she says softly, sorrowfully.

Yes, I am stupidly brave at times and speak when I should be silent, but now I am struck dumb.

The Black Crow envies the Little Bird? How can that be...?

"Aaaa-yeeeee! No! Help!"

At the sound of girlish screams, we all turn in haste to see *who* is alarmed and the *manner* of the alarm.

Father and Mr Palmer-Reeves have heard it too, and are striding at some speed from the spring grass slopes.

Even Lachlan and the pup stop in their game of fetch-the-stick and stare.

"Get it away from me! Someone, please!"

The voice is so very desperate and earnest in its fear

that truly you would think something close to murder had befallen its owner.

But when I see Miss Kitty stumble out of our house, flapping at a startled chicken who is flapping back, I can do only one awful thing.

I laugh, and cannot stop.

I laugh, at the silliness of this girl in her bonnet and frills.

I laugh, because how can anyone not when the cause of the commotion is just a daft bundle of feathers with no more malice in it than the puffball of a dandelion?

And then I see Father's face as he draws closer – the look of it is so solemn and strange that my laughter catches in my throat.

Something is *so* very, very wrong in this moment, and it has nothing to do with the fussing miss in her finery who is now glowering my way.

CHAPTER 9

Hello…

I see the dream is here.

I find myself atop the Crags. The never-ending sky so low, so close that I might touch it.

With joy filling me to my fingertips, I stand, bare tiptoes on the bed of soft moss, stretch my arms out wide and tilt backwards, as if I am angel-born, about to make my bed on the drifting, fluffy cloud that now skirts and flits by me.

And I will be happy, so very happy to let the westerly wind lift and glide myself and my cloud-bed to wherever it fancies. I have no fear where that might be, for soon the comforting hand will slip into mine and I will trust it to keep me safe…

Only the wind has a wildness to it, my cloud-bed buffets and bumps me.

The fingers of my weak hand reach for the guiding hand … but it is not there. There is nothing there.

There is nothing anywhere. No cloud-bed beneath

me, no sun to warm me, no America in the distance, no island below me.

There is only the sound of dark thunder and I am falling, falling, falling.

And calling, calling, calling my sisters' names.

"Oh!" I gasp, and sit upright in the bed, with the slumbering bodies of Ishbel and Effie on either side of me, I am relieved to see.

The hour is very early, I think. For a moment I long for the wakeful company of my sisters, however bossy they are, so that the loneliness of my dream can be shooed away. But Ishbel and Effie were so alarmed and laid low by Father's news yesterday that I only wish them the comfort of their undisturbed sleep before the day's work calls them.

Luckily, the fine summer weather meant the doors of the box bed were left open overnight, and I am calmed by the sight of sunlight spilling across the floor of our room. In no time at all, the queerness of my dreaming drifts away, before it has a chance to feel like some omen that Effie would believe in, I think to myself.

Turning my back on my middle sister and her tousle of red hair, I slowly lift myself up and over the sleeping form of Ishbel, her long black plait like a dozing snake on the pillow. My stronger foot stretches down for the cold firmness of the flagstones Father laid with such care so long ago, while we – such small versions of ourselves, my sisters and I – watched with fascination at his speed and skill and strength. How proud Mother looked, coming to join us with Lachlan wrapped small and safe in her plaid shawl.

But today, nothing feels safe any more.

For yesterday, the Laird did not come just to converse with Father for politeness' sake. What he did was look over our well-built home and well-run croft and deem it so very, *very* good a place that Father must pay much, *much* more rent for the privilege of continuing to live here!

"Bridie?"

Father's voice calls to me softly, as I clutch my billowing nightgown and pitter-patter into the main room.

I had thought to be useful. To quietly make the fire up and set the dishes for breakfast and have the porridge simmering before anyone else awoke. To make a little comfort this morning when it felt like comfort was a thing flown last night.

But here is Father now, sitting in his chair by the flickering fire, up before any of us. Though I notice he is full dressed, boots and all. Perhaps he has not been to bed! He does have a dark-eyed look of someone who might have stayed awake all night. I could imagine that is so. I could imagine the Laird's words would be rattling around his head. I could imagine what the other menfolk of our township thought when Father went off to meet with them after the Laird took his leave…

"Hello, Father. Is there tea? Shall I make you some?"

It is a small thing to say. What I really want to ask I cannot, in case it injures him more to think of the decision he was told of yesterday.

"Come here, Bridie," Father says softly, and pats one leg. I am grateful for the offer to sit there and have his arms around me. And I am grateful for being small for my age so that I can nestle in and feel the comforting pound of his heart and the rough brush of his beard as he plants a kiss on my forehead.

"Must you really go away, Father?" I ask him.

I know that he must. He said so yesterday, did he not? He will not touch the money put away in Mother's tin box in the eaves, so it is decided that he will take work on the mainland till harvest at the end of summer. That we will just have to manage without him while he earns extra. Some of the township menfolk will help us, he says, if the work is too heavy for us. But I do not say what is truly on my mind – that if the Laird is prepared to put up *our* rent, then he will no doubt be telling the same to our neighbours by and by. And then *their* menfolk will have to find work away too.

For certain, Tornish will eventually be townships of old folk, women and children. All of us left would have our wits and determination, all of us would pull together, but the loss of the strongest men for the weightier tasks around the crofts will make life that bit harder than it often is already.

"Yes, there really is nothing else, my dear," says Father, resting his cheek on the top of my head. "But I will not go straightaway. I will tell the ferryman to put word out that I am looking for stone-work. And till then I will do what needs doing and mend what needs mending so you are left in a good position here."

"We will be just grand," I tell him, for I know that is what he needs to hear.

"I have no doubt you will," Father replies with a crack in his voice. He quickly coughs to clear it and more robustly adds, "Now, off with you and see if those hens have an egg for my breakfast!"

Of course I do as I am bid.

And later, after we are all dressed and breakfasted and about our business, I find myself in the company of the hens again, this time chasing them away from the wooden tub of oatmeal I sit grinding in the sunshine of the yard.

Father is long gone, off to check the crops. Ishbel left an hour since for the Big House. And Effie is fiercely beating the straw mattresses flat and cleaning everything in our cottage as if that will make all well, so I am happy to be out of her way, happy that soon Lachlan and myself can escape. For Will should be here very soon, and Mr Samuel too. Before the Laird's party left yesterday, after the daft little chicken frightened Miss Kitty so, Mr Samuel was very firm again in his wishes to tour the island. And to start, he bid me take him to my favourite spot this very morning.

And where else would that be but the top of the Glas Crags? I do not know if Mr Samuel plans to take his easel contraption and his bags and boxes of paint too, but between the young gentleman, Will, myself and Lachlan, we will manage to get the equipment to the top of the—

The sound of voices joined in chatter causes me to look up from my pounding of oatmeal and scolding of silly chickens.

And there, coming towards me, is a surprising grouping of folk.

I am not so surprised that Will and Mr Samuel have met up and walked in harmonious companionship.

I am surprised at who walks with them.

For it is the Black Crow, Miss Tulliver, with her grumpy maidservant Maude stomping behind.

"Little Bird! Look who I found on the way!" Will calls out, though I know my good friend must have waited and sought out Mr Samuel deliberately, since his township is in the opposite direction of the Big House.

"And look who has come to take the air and see the sights this beautiful morning!" Mr Samuel calls out, nodding his head at the shrouded lady whose black arm is linked in his maroon-coated one. "I found Miss Tulliver taking a turn around the gardens, and she was most intrigued by our plans for the day. At first she was a little shy at the thought of accompanying me, but when I pointed out that she would have not one but *four* chaperones, she was quite persuaded."

I don't have enough English to know all of the words Mr Samuel uses but I can guess at their meaning; at "chaperone", he motioned at Maude, myself, Will and Lachlan, so I suppose he means that our presence makes it decent for Miss Tulliver to be in his company.

Speaking of Maude, the maidservant is trailing behind, glowering at the back of Mr Samuel's head as he talks. My sister Effie is sweetly plump of cheek, but this miss is of a largeness and with such an ill-humoured manner that makes me think she would rather stay home and look at four walls than tramp around the countryside. She for one will not be scrambling up the Glas Crags this fine morning, decency or not.

But then, I think perhaps that none of us will be. Miss Tulliver is surely too ladylike to come clambering the Crags...

"Good morning, Mr Samuel, good morning, miss," I say, as I get to my feet and put a lid over the oatmeal. "Can I ... can I get you some tea?"

"Tea?" says Mr Samuel with a frown and a smile. "Thank you, no. I hoped you would be ready to show us the view from your special hill, Little Bird?"

"She is! We are!" Will replies brightly, and goes to continue on.

"But, sir," I say to Mr Samuel, "you have no painting things."

"*This* is all I need for today," says Mr Samuel, patting the book in his pocket that he had with him inside our cottage yesterday.

"But – but Miss Tulliver might not be of a mind to climb to such a height," I add, more to the point.

"Ah, but you are wrong there," Mr Samuel says with a wide grin. "For when I told Miss Tulliver our plans, she was *very* keen to come."

"When I was young, before my father died, my parents and I often took walking tours in the Lake District," says the soft, girlish voice from behind the veil. "I would very much like to do something like that again."

Where and what is the Lake District, I wonder? Before I can ask, there comes a mumbling from behind Mr Samuel and Miss Tulliver.

"I'm sorry, Maude, did you say something?" Mr Samuel asks, turning to speak to the maidservant with an unexpectedly cool countenance, for one who I have previously only seen smiling.

The maid tilts her chin up defiantly. "I said I shall *not* go up that hill. You cannot make me."

"No one is making you," says Mr Samuel, with a

touch of steel in his voice. "I'm sure you can wait here."

"Of course," I hurriedly agree. "Please have this stool, miss, and my brother can get you water."

As I look around and see Lachlan hurrying towards us, I lift my hand and point to the water bucket so he understands my meaning. At the same time, I hear the maid's complaining voice again.

"Very well. But Miss *Tulliver* should not be going either. She did not ask permission."

I turn to see that timid Miss Tulliver must now be a little vexed, as the black lace of her veil puffs out as she speaks her next words. "Who would you have me ask permission of, Maude? The Master is out around the island this morning visiting some of his tenants, and the Mistress and Miss Kitty will not rise for two hours or more yet."

Maude the maid looks chastened yet furious at Miss Tulliver's words.

Mr Samuel, I suppose, is neither a servant nor gentry. It would not be done for him to tell Miss Tulliver that he is pleased she has spoken up for herself. But the small smile he gives her says as much as any words might.

As for Will and I … we look at each other in alarm. From what Miss Tulliver says, can we expect that her guardian is delivering news of rent increases to *more* of the islanders…?

"Then it is fixed. Shall we be off?" says Mr Samuel,

once more in a genial tone.

And so I set aside my task, and once Lachlan warily offers a tin cup of water to the sulky Maude, we all set off. On reaching the first, gentle green slope at the foot of the Crags, I turn to see Maude perched on the tiny stool, staring after us. She is unaware that she herself is being stared at; by Effie, who is poised with hands on hips in the cottage doorway, finished with pummelling the mattresses and now no doubt wondering what this maid is doing sitting in our yard.

Effie may not be best pleased to find herself with an unexpected and ungrateful guest, but she will do her duty and make sure the girl is comfortable enough while we are gone.

And I must do my duty and take the Laird's guest and ward where they wish to go, though it takes longer than usual. Where Will and I would scamper straight up the jumbled, uneven steps of rocks, this morning we must take the more meandering paths worn by the feet of sheep and goats, which are easier – though not by much – for Miss Tulliver's voluminous skirts.

But perhaps the longer route makes the arrival at the summit all the more of a reward.

"Oh, my!" gasps Miss Tulliver, as we stand on the flat place with its carpeting of moss and a view that takes your breath away – even mine, with all the times I've viewed it.

"Here, I will name for you the places and mountains you can see!" Will tells Miss Tulliver, as they walk forward to face the mainland, with its ragged, great fingers of rocks reaching out towards us and the grandeur of the mountain ranges in the distance. Lachlan happily follows them, like a puppy in boy form.

Mr Samuel hangs back a little, though, so I keep him company. He is taking his book out of his pocket, and a pencil too. He flicks through to a page that is clean and new and free of marks – and immediately begins to draw. But he does not draw the view of sea and sky and towering peaks as you may expect; with a few short strokes he captures the form of Miss Tulliver, of her tiny waist and billowing skirts. Of her hand lifted in wonder to her mouth that is hidden behind the trailing veil.

"How can you do that?" I ask him, since such an image appearing so quickly seems almost magical to me.

"Because I love to capture people when they are at their most natural," says Mr Samuel, his eyes darting from his book to his subject and back again. "It is so much more of a pleasure than doing stiff portraits, though they are what pays my rent."

"You are not enjoying painting the Laird, then?" I ask, as I watch his pencil dart about the white page.

"I am not enjoying painting the Laird, no. He makes it quite clear that I am a nuisance he must put up with for the sake of his vanity," Mr Samuel mutters as he concentrates. "But at least I need only stay a short while here; long enough to do my work and be paid for it. Poor Miss Tulliver is treated in the household as just as much of a nuisance, but she is forever bound to stay with her unwelcoming guardian and his family."

From what little I have so far heard and seen, I would suppose Miss Tulliver is not held in particularly high regard by the Palmer-Reeveses, but it is quite a shock to hear Mr Samuel talk so bold on the matter. In fact, I am so startled at Mr Samuel's disclosure that it overshadows the sharp stab of disappointment at his mention of staying but a short while on Tornish.

"They do not treat her at all kindly?" I ask, watching as Miss Tulliver tilts her head back and laughs at something foolish and pleasing that my silly William has said to her.

Perhaps this is why Miss Tulliver said she envied me yesterday. She saw that despite our small home and careless state of dress, me and my family are hearty and happy, while she plainly is not…

"The family *and* their staff treat the little dog with more regard than Miss Tulliver," says Mr Samuel. "And they do not treat *it* with much regard at all. But now come; I wish to draw you again, Little Bird. Can you sit, perhaps, on that rock there?"

I do not move. "What do you mean, draw me 'again'?" I challenge him.

Smiling, Mr Samuel flicks to an earlier page in his

book … and there I am, and there are my sisters, just a few flicks and gestures but clearly us. The figure crouched by the fire with a kettle is Ishbel, while Effie and I, hair loose and long, stand sentinel either side of the fireplace, as if we are mimicking the china dogs on the mantle. Mr Samuel must have drawn us unnoticed as he sat on the settle yesterday afternoon!

"Do you like it?" he asks.

"Of course!" I tell him, and before another second passes, the page is neatly ripped from the book and passed to me.

"A gift," Mr Samuel says simply. "Now, please do me this favour, Little Bird, and sit over there so I can capture you while that pleasing cluster of clouds is in my eyeline."

Oh, my … I am to be drawn, I *have* been drawn, by an artist!

I do hope the darting breeze cools the pools of red I feel burning on my cheeks as I slip atop the boulder. Pulling my feet up beside me, I place one hand on the hard surface to support me, while my weaker left hand lays in my lap, resting on the large pocket of my apron wherein lies the gift of the picture I have just been given.

"Will this do?" I ask shyly, wishing I had tied my hair neat this morning, so that it would not dance and slap around my face and shoulders.

"It will indeed," Mr Samuel says. "A little bird with

nothing but an empty horizon behind…"

"But, sir, it is *not* empty," I reply. "If I had wings to take me, I would fly in that direction, all the way west and not stop till I was at the shore of America!"

"America?" says Miss Tulliver, hearing our conversation and turning to see that I – a scrawny, ordinary girl – am now *muse* to Mr Samuel. "Oh, I too wish I could see that country! They have a song there that describes it as 'the land of the free'. What a thought, eh?"

I suddenly, desperately wish it was possible to look Miss Tulliver full in the face, for in this instant I feel a unity between us. Our paths in life are quite different, but I think we both have a burning desire for a freedom that girls and women – rich or poor – can never have.

"But why would anyone want to live anywhere but this glorious island?" Will bursts in, laughing at the very idea of another sort of place or another sort of life.

His lust and laughter is infectious, and we all laugh too. Till a harsh, chill gust of wind rushes at us from the Atlantic. It slaps hard against my back, makes the pages of Mr Samuel's book flap and crackle and near tear, and causes Miss Tulliver to cry out sharply – for the gust has lifted her carefully pinned veil clean off her head and sent it flying into the air.

Miss Tulliver is turned half away from us, watching her panel of lace tumble in the breeze and Lachlan jumping in a failed bid to catch it. In that fleeting moment, I see her hair is the colour of dark honey, and pulled back to a tight bun at the nape of her neck. And the age she must be … twenty-one or two or three, I guess. Around the same as Mr Samuel, perhaps?

But that is not all I see. In the next moment she turns to Will, Mr Samuel and myself with a look of sheer terror in her new-seen eyes; large, blinking eyes in a heart-shaped face that is on one side as milky-pale as you would expect for skin hidden each and every day from the sun. But the other side of her face is a very different hue; a vivid pink, like that of the skin on her wrist. And like her wrist, the skin is puckered and pulled into the odd wrinkles caused by burning.

"Oh!" whimpers Miss Tulliver, slapping her hands across the damaged side. She seems to stumble a little, as if the wind is too strong for her, or as if she might faint at the shock of being so forcefully unveiled before us.

Will – standing at her side – quickly puts an arm around Miss Tulliver's waist and guides her to the boulder I sit on, lest her legs give out beneath her. Of course, I shuffle over to make space.

"Miss Tulliver! Caroline!" Mr Samuel calls out, hastily shoving his book in his pocket. He bounds over to us, and kneels in front of the trembling lady beside me. "Please, please … do not fret so. You are with friends."

He reaches his hand to Miss Tulliver's, and gently peels her fingers away from the side of her face that she is covering.

"No, no … I am so ugly!" she protests, though she does not wrestle her shaking fingers from Mr Samuel's grasp.

"Not at all!" says Mr Samuel earnestly.

For a second my mind whirls with the notion that Miss Tulliver must have burns all down her right side; the puckered wrinkles are on her neck too, and no doubt travel their meandering way down her arm to her wrist.

And then the wind quietens as quick as it came, and my thoughts clear. We have something else in common, Miss Tulliver and I.

"Miss, you look fine indeed," I say to her. "You just have a few marks, that is all. Just as I am like every other girl, but lack a little strength here and there."

Miss Tulliver turns to look at me as I wave my weak hand and point the toes of my twisted foot, her eyes brimming with tears while a small smile falters and flickers on her lips.

"I hardly think people would look upon me and call these 'just a few marks'…" she says.

"And should people describe them aloud in any other terms," Will says stoutly, "then they would be rude fools!"

"Indeed!" Mr Samuel agrees earnestly. "Our friends Little Bird and Will are very wise, Caroline!"

I feel my cheeks colour – what a strange and pleasant thing it is to be called a friend to these fine and good people!

"Yes, yes they are," says Miss Tulliver, looking particularly upon me.

And now I think I understand why she said she envied me yesterday. She feels – or has been *made* to feel – that her burns are something shameful. And she has come to see that I feel no shame at all in *my* small differences to others.

"Well, I think you are very pretty!" says Lachlan, who has quickly gathered a little beauty for Miss Tulliver; he drops puffs of yellow blossom from the jagged gorse on to the black wool lap of her skirts.

Miss Tulliver – or may I now think of her in more warm terms, as Miss Caroline? – begins to say a pleased and surprised thank you, when a new voice utters her name.

"Miss Tulliver? Miss Tulliver?"

We all turn to see someone who has not come to the top of the Glas Crags for the last three years, for Effie set aside any playfulness and wonder when Mother died.

But most peculiarly, my sister has chosen to climb its heights now, with her skirts clutched in bunches in her hand.

"Effie!" Lachlan calls out, rushing over to her. "Why are you here?"

Effie pauses a minute to fill her panting lungs with air and – I can tell – quiet her surprise at seeing Miss Caroline without her mask of veil and with her face marked with her history.

"If you please," she says directly to Miss Tulliver, "I have been sent to fetch you by the Laird. He came riding by and saw your maid. He bids you come down from the Crags immediately, lest you fall and hurt yourself, or worse. You are told to return home straightaway."

With the skirl of the wind, Miss Tulliver's soft-spoken words are almost lost ... but I can make them out.

"I think that my uncle might prefer it, if it were 'worse'..."

With those muttered words, she gets to her feet, letting the blossom of gorse tumble to the ground.

All happiness and hope seem drained from her now dulled eyes, I see.

While behind her, in the blue distance, the gusting wind speeds off westwards with her dancing lace veil.

CHAPTER 10

Victoria, sovereign Queen of Great Britain and Ireland, is the most important woman in the land – one of the most important women in the whole of the world, I am told.

But she is *tiny*, Mr Samuel says. Small as a child. Small as *me*, he supposes, having once seen her in Edinburgh, when she visited. I too have seen the Queen, but only in drawings and photographs printed in the newspapers that Father has brought back with him on the ferry from the mainland.

Can you believe it? I hardly can, but tomorrow I will see for myself if this is true, for a steamship is to arrive here on Tornish with Her Majesty, her German husband Prince Albert, their family and whatever retinue might travel with a royal party! The royals are headed to their Scottish summer home – Balmoral Castle, it is called – but have chosen to visit some of the islands of the west coast beforehand.

"Are you managing there, Bridie?" Fergus Matheson

calls down to me and Lachlan from the loaded cart he is driving past us on the lane from the harbour. Beside him is his brother Donal, who gives us a smile and a nod.

"Aye, we are fine," I tell him, as together my own brother and I push a heavy barrow-load of wrapped hams and such that have been loaded off the ferry just now. Will has already gone ahead, helping his brother George take a creel of lobsters to the kitchens of the Laird's house. And I fancy that though Donal and Fergus despise Mr Palmer-Reeves, they will be pleased enough to deliver the stuff he has ordered, so that they may catch a glimpse of Ishbel at her work...

"So will we have a race now to the Big House?" Fergus jokes, pitting his hardy horse and cart against Lachlan and I, barefoot and only *just* managing a barrow handle each.

"Tell you what, we will give you a head start," I joke back, nodding for them to be on their way with the Laird's stuff.

Both the young men laugh good-naturedly at my cheek, then trundle off ahead of us.

"Bridie, will the Queen wear her crown and jewels?" asks Lachlan, as the dust kicked up by the cartwheels drifts in sunlit flurries ahead of us. Behind us, I hear the high-pitched voices of some of our neighbour's children, giggling and carrying goods as we are doing.

LITTLE BIRD FLIES

It is lucky for the Laird — if not for the education of the island's children — that the school is still shut; it means there are many hands available to help shift ashore such a vast amount of things that appear to be necessary for such a small Queen's visit...

"No, I think Queen Victoria will be dressed quite modestly, in country clothes," I tell Lachlan, since Mr Samuel has told me this himself. When relaxing in the Highlands, Her Majesty likes to set aside the finery she must wear as her duty, Mr Samuel said yesterday, while he sketched Lachlan running, his skinny chest bare, back and forth beneath the waterfall that lies at the most southerly point of Tornish. (The drawing is a marvel, and even better than the one he did the day before, of Will and I by the ancient Standing Stones on the moor.)

"Oh," says Lachlan, sounding a little disappointed and then perking up again as a new notion comes to him. "It must be very nice for her children, to have a mother who is so special."

I notice that as my brother talks, he does not see that we are passing the churchyard where our own mother lies. It is difficult for Lachlan; he feels her loss because Mother died when he was little enough to be held and hugged by her in a way that my sisters had outgrown. And then it is *easier* for him in a way too; the past has a hazy quality to it for younger children, does it not? As if events were just a story; as if Mother may have been just a character in a tale Lachlan once heard.

"Indeed, the lives of the royal children must be very pleasant," I agree, as I steer the barrow here and there so that we do not fall into the ruts that criss-cross the lane. "But remember, not all of the children are young, Lachlan. Some are nearly grown men and women now!"

"Oh, yes…" he says, sounding disappointed. I think he imagines children always staying children. But Queen Victoria has not only ruled her country for almost a quarter of a century but had nine sons and daughters spanning that time too.

As we steer our load towards the left fork that leads to the approach to the Big House, Lachlan once again brightens up. He chatters and chirps, wondering what Prince Leopold will look like (since he is the closest to Lachlan's age), whether we might see the Queen out and about the island, whether she might stop to take tea at our cottage, do I know how very low he must bow to her…?

I manage an answer here and there, but really, I am lost in my own thoughts. Lately, everything has been such a queer mix: truly the best of times and the worst.

One of the best? Well, I am so very glad and grateful to have had the keen pleasure of knowing such a kind, interesting gentleman as Mr Samuel. I swear the last few days where we have taken him around the island have been some of my happiest. He has spoken of artists he admires, and described to me their paintings, so that I can almost picture them in my mind's eye. He has told me of the majestic cathedral and university buildings of Glasgow, and the strange-sounding graveyard there that is big as a village, with its residents all at their rest in the ground! But the worst of it is the reason for Mr Samuel's presence; he would not be here if Mr Palmer-Reeves had not become the new Laird. And having Mr Palmer-Reeves among us is akin to having a storm-cloud settle over Tornish; a storm-cloud that darkens with every day that goes by.

And of course I am glad and grateful for the hateful schoolmaster Mr Simpson taking his leave, so that Will and I and Lachlan have been able to spend our days showing Mr Samuel the best of the island. But then it seems the Laird has as much interest in finding a new teacher for the children of his tenants as he has to furnish their cattle with pretty bonnets – and this lack of care and thought does not endear him to the islanders.

Also, I am glad and grateful for catching a glimpse of the young woman behind the guise of the Black Crow. But for four days now I have not set eyes on Miss Tulliver. Since the morning she scaled the Glas Crags, she has been ordered to stay home, and not to leave the grounds of the Big House unless she is in the company of the Laird or the Mistress. This news comes direct from Mr Samuel, who has contrived to speak with her often while she circles the gardens like a restless caged animal, with a new, heavier, plainer veil that has been made for her.

And now the Queen ... how wonderful will it be to stand at the harbour tomorrow and see this famed, all-powerful woman come to our quiet corner of the Highlands! Tomorrow truly will be the best of times. And I do not want to seem like Effie with her superstitions, but should I expect the worst of times to come hand in hand?

"Quick," I say to Lachlan, as we go through the huge iron entrance gates. "We should not be seen by the family..."

And so we make haste, following the path around the side of the building that will bring us to the courtyard at the back. For once, I wish that the old Laird had done as other Big Houses do and have a gated entrance there just for the servants, so that we would not feel this pressure to be invisible to those who might stare out of the curtained windows at the front of the house.

But as we trundle and steer our way towards the yard, a streak of fur rushes towards us.

"It is the little dog! Patch!" Lachlan cries out in delight – till Patch neatly snatches a leg of ham that is practically the same size as him. It bounces along the ground as he runs off with it towards the front of the house.

Thumping his side of the barrow down, Lachlan goes in chase – and I am uncertain what to do. Go in chase as well? But I would be better to struggle and push the barrow round to the kitchens than leave it here unattended.

So with a deep breath, I try to lift both handles; but the weight of it is too much for my weak hand and it clatters down with a sharp crack of wood. Luckily, the sound is heard by someone who can help; Donal Matheson sticks his head around the corner of the building and, seeing me in need, comes towards me. He must have been chatting to Ishbel, for she quickly hurries after him.

And now someone *else* shows interest in my plight; a window very close is flung open, the room Ishbel has told me is the library … and after a moment of alarm, I see with relief that it is Mr Samuel.

"You look like a street trader, Little Bird!" he says with his usual easy smile. "I could well imagine you on the wide roads of Glasgow, selling your wares!"

My chest swells at the thought of that. What a job to have! To watch the hustle and bustle of coaches and horses passing by, of talking to more customers in an hour than I talk to all week here on Tornish!

But then my eyes suddenly alight on something

directly behind Mr Samuel, and I move closer to the windowsill to view it. It is the Laird's portrait.

"Oh, would you like to see how it is coming along?" asks Mr Samuel, and he steps back inside the book-filled room, so he can turn the easel a little and give me a better view of the painting.

I am surprised. Not by the figure I see, but by what he stands in front of.

"What made you choose the woods?" I ask in surprise, as I frown at the image of the tweed-suited, twirl-moustached Mr Palmer-Reeves, with a dense, dark forest behind him. Did Will and I and Lachlan not take Mr Samuel to see the very best scenery the island had to offer, any of which he might have chosen to paint in the background?

"Well, I told the Laird that the strength of the trees suited his character. But in truth? He didn't deserve the loveliness you showed me," says Mr Samuel, lowering his voice and smiling wryly.

"You have his likeness very well," says Ishbel, joining me at the window.

"Yes, you have made him seem just as overly proud and mean-spirited as he is," says Donal Matheson, deserting the barrow as I have done, to get a glimpse of the work Mr Samuel has been so diligently perfecting.

"Shush!" says Ishbel, hitting her beau on the arm, her tone worried and warning. "What if the Laird hears?"

Donal responds by planting a quick kiss on her cheek, and saying, "Don't you worry; I'm too clever to get caught by the likes of him!"

Another time, I would be as surprised as Ishbel at Donal's brazenness. But I am too upset by what I see before me. The painting; it looks so very nearly finished. And if that is so, then Mr Samuel will be taking his leave of us, and packing his things to go back to Glasgow and—

"Donal!" comes a shout, as Fergus clatters up to us with his solid-shouldered workhorse and now-empty cart. Empty of goods, that is: now George and Will, their lobsters put away in the kitchens, are hitching a lift away home, or perhaps back to the harbour. I give Will a quick smile – but he gives me nothing but the strangest of looks in return. What is that about? We are to meet later; Mr Samuel wishes us to show him the distant lochan this afternoon. I will find out then what troubles my friend.

"But I am helping Bridie with this…" Donal's words fade as he looks, as Ishbel and I do, at the tight-lipped, angry faces of his brother and George. "Sorry, Bridie. I must go."

And with another quick kiss planted on a startled Ishbel's cheek, Donal leaps up on to the cart, and he and his brother and the others hare away as if the very devil were after them.

Ishbel and I turn to watch them go, and both start when we see the Mistress herself glowering at us from the corner at the front of the house.

"You – a word, please," she says, ushering Ishbel to her.

I hang back, not sure what to do as Ishbel walks towards the Mistress, her dark head bowed low…

"Here, let me help you with that," I hear Mr Samuel say, and turn to see him jump down from the open long window, and bound over to lift the handles of my barrow. He is not expecting it to be so heavy I think, and as he lifts it, the barrow tilts to one side – I leap to his aid as he has leapt to mine, and catch a ham before it rolls to the ground.

"How hungry does Mr Palmer-Reeves think the Queen will be?" Mr Samuel jokes, as we lurch towards the back of the house, him steering our way, myself keeping a hand on our unsteady load. "Perhaps he hopes for some royal favour. A knighthood for a ham! Or—"

Mr Samuel halts in his jesting as two sleek giants clip-clop towards us from the direction of the stables; Mr Palmer-Reeves is riding the finer of the two horses, with his lawyer friend Mr Jenkins astride the other. The two men might normally think themselves above everyone, and today, from their lofty heights, they do not even seem to acknowledge those busy on the ground on their behalf. And so they converse as if their worthy voices will not drift down to us mortals below; us mortals who know very little English beyond commands, they stupidly think. In fact these "gentlemen" are so stupid, so careless, so taken with their own self-importance that they do not even notice that Mr Samuel is among our ranks.

"…as Kitty says, Her Majesty will hardly want to be introduced to such a drab creature!" Mr Palmer-Reeves guffaws.

"Shall you order her to keep to her quarters while the Queen visits?" asks Mr Jenkins.

"Yes, it's for the best," says the Laird, as they pass us. "Oh, if only I could marry the damned woman off and be done with it. But who decent would have her?"

I glance at Mr Samuel and he meets my gaze; he knows, as I do, that the "gentlemen" can be talking of one person only.

"Listen," I hear Mr Jenkins say, as their steeds clip-clop towards the front gardens and entrance gates, "I've told you before, there is *another* way to deal with your burden, and it's one that's far better for you. I have all the details of the place at Gartnavel. One signature from you and…"

They are gone from us, or at least far enough away that we cannot catch the remainder of their words.

"What are they talking about?" I whisper to Mr Samuel, as my mind translates the English words as best it can. "What does 'gartnavel' mean?"

"It is an area in Glasgow," Mr Samuel answers, frowning. "I cannot think what place they refer to there…"

With the curiousness of the overheard conversation, we have stalled in our walking, I realise – Ishbel has just hurried past us, looking neither left nor right about her.

"Ishbel? Ishbel!" I call out, and scamper after my sister, leaving the barrow and Mr Samuel behind me.

She carries on walking at speed, heading for the back of the house and the kitchens, even when I come in front of her.

"Ishbel?" I say again, grabbing hold of her arm to slow her. "What is the matter?"

At last she halts, and I see that her dark eyes are pooled with tears.

"I am to work till the Queen's visit is done, and then I am dismissed," she says in a tremulous voice, not able to meet my eyes.

"Dismissed? What for?" I gasp.

"For disgraceful and disgusting behaviour, the Mistress says," Ishbel replies.

I shake my head, understanding nothing. How could my graceful, well-mannered sister be described this way? And then I guess at the truth of it…

"Because Donal stole a kiss from you?" I ask, knowing this must be the answer.

Ishbel nods and tries to say yes, but the word is stuck in her throat. With a cough, she takes her leave of me, muttering, "I must go about my business or I will not get my final wages…"

"What is happening, Little Bird?" Mr Samuel asks as he and the wobbly barrow catch me up. He awaits my explanation, but I cannot give him one as a sudden *new* sound has struck further fear into my heart.

The barking is incessant, and I remember that Lachlan is somewhere around the front of the house, chasing after Patch with his prize. Knowing the Mistress to be in the foulest of moods, I do not want my brother to cross paths with her.

So I scurry back the way I came (darting sideways to avoid another horse and laden cart that comes careering through the gates) and glance quickly around.

And there – there is the scene I did not wish to see.

Over by some ornamental flowering bush stands a panting Lachlan, clutching the ham, while Patch the dog barks and jumps, half playing, half disappointed at the loss of his thieved treat.

The Mistress, shouting, "Stop where you are!" is bearing down on my brother, her heeled shoes crunching on the stones of the driveway.

"Don't worry, Mother! I have him!" cries a shrill voice, and Miss Kitty comes out from under an arched bower of roses, where she must have been sitting.

She rushes towards Lachlan with clipped but forceful steps, one of those tiny fool's umbrellas dipping up and down above her head. The look of her is so comical I almost feel like laughing, till she reaches up and pulls the umbrella flat to its stick – and transforms it into a dainty club…

Without a word, but with teeth gritted like a wolfhound who has cornered a rabbit, Miss Kitty lifts the club she has made and brings it down hard.

In that second, before the shock hits me, I feel so very foolish. For at first I thought it cruel of her to hit the small dog, until I realised her aim was not *meant* for Patch. The blow hits my brother's cheek with a resounding whack, causing him to stagger and drop the rescued leg of ham.

"Lachlan!" I call out, grabbing my skirts as I hasten towards him, for once cursing my bad foot for slowing my progress.

But I think the blow has left Lachlan reeling with fright; like a wild beast, it is as if he thinks flight is his only path, and without looking my way, he turns and runs, runs through the open gates, darting between men carrying sacks across their backs.

I go to follow my little brother, but not before I see Miss Kitty stare my way. Perhaps I might have hoped to see her contrite, shocked at what she has done in the spur of the moment. Instead she is like some half-crazed creature, her eyes glazed with something like hate or delight, I cannot tell which.

Then she gives me a slow-spreading smile that curdles my blood.

And in that moment, I feel my family is quite undone.

CHAPTER 11

The lochan is the most peaceful spot on the island, its still waters ringed by the raggedy beauty of Scots pines.

But those gathered around it this afternoon have no peace in their hearts. The only one that is content is Patch, who Will came across in the woods that back on to the Big House this afternoon as he waited for Mr Samuel. The dog abandoned what was left of his stolen goods and followed Will and Mr Samuel here, despite their urging him home. He is now lying near Lachlan, sleeping off his bellyful of ill-gotten ham, while Lachlan lies with his head in Effie's lap.

It was a surprise to me that our sister joined us here this afternoon. But I think she had no taste nor energy for chores, not once her anger and tears were eventually spent over the sight of the weal on Lachlan's cheek and the news of Ishbel's dismissal. Indeed, a listlessness came over her and she trailed along with Lachlan and myself to the lochan. Since we arrived she has sat staring at the rippling water, stroking Lachlan's still head and softly singing, "*A ghaoil, leig dhachaigh gum mhàthair mi…*"

"*Love, let me home to my mother…*"

The way that she is, I am not sure Effie is even *aware* that she is singing, let along *what* she is singing. It is a very old song about a young girl in danger, which seems fitting for this moment, after the news Will told me when he called for me at the cottage earlier, on his way to meet Mr Samuel. For is not every Tornish girl in danger, along with every boy, man and woman who calls the island their home?

"So your father does not yet know what has befallen your sister and brother, Bridie?" asks Mr Samuel, taking a seat upon a tree stump.

"He is gone to the furthest west township to advise them of the Laird's intentions to increase rents," I tell him, "so no, he does not yet know."

"And *you* do not know the worst of it, Mr Samuel," says Will, balancing on his haunches as his hand searches out stones in the shingle by the water's edge. "I dared not tell you till we were far from the Big House and any crofts as we walked here."

"What is it, Will?" Mr Samuel asks with a concerned frown. "I cannot believe you have *worse* news to tell me?"

Will stands, shoots me a look and shrugs as he tells his tale to our gentleman friend.

"Aye, it's worse. Before Fergus left the yard earlier,

he took his horse to the water trough and overheard some lads talking; the groom and another of the Laird's London staff," says Will, breaking his story every few words to angrily skim stone after flat stone over the water's surface. "It seems the Laird's plan is to raise rents *so* high that tenants will eventually come to realise they cannot pay what he asks and so will begin to leave the island, having no other choice, and no means to survive. In the meantime, Mr Palmer-Reeves is to arrange to have a herd of deer brought across from the mainland to breed."

"*Deer?*" Mr Samuel splutters in surprise. "From what I know of the sad history of this part of Scotland, I thought you to mean *sheep* were to soon be farmed here for their wool. What good are *deer?*"

"Deer may have no wool to sell, but they can certainly make the Laird money," Will continues, a dark rage boiling just under his skin, I can tell. "For this time next spring, Tornish will be but a sporting ground for rich folk to come shoot the stags and hinds at will on what once was our crofts and pastures…"

Mr Samuel drops his head into his hands.

"So help me … I *cannot* stay in that house, with those people, a day longer," he moans. "That they can treat dear Miss Caroline the way they do; that they can treat your family the way they have today; that Mr Palmer-Reeves can have so little regard for his tenants… I tell you I would forgo my fee for the painting and throw the wretched thing on the fire, if I could get off this accursed island before the ferry comes again next week!"

"Please, sir. I beg you, do not talk of our home that way," says Effie, suddenly stirring. "It is not the island that is accursed, but the people who now call themselves our Laird and Mistress!"

"Forgive me, Effie; my temper led me astray," Mr Samuel apologises. "I did not mean to slander this perfect place. I only…"

The darkness suddenly lifts from his brow, and his eyes open wide in shock.

"I have it now, Little Bird! I *know* what Mr Jenkins spoke of when he and the Laird rode by," he mutters, turning to me. "Gartnavel … the lunatic asylum is there!"

"What is this?" asks Effie, looking from Mr Samuel to me, and understanding as little of the English words as I do.

"It is where they send people…" Mr Samuel casts around for something we might understand "… people who have quite lost their minds!"

"But Miss Tulliver is not like that," I say urgently. "Her only trouble is that she grieves still for her mother, and feels she must hide her scars from prying eyes. On what grounds would the Laird's lawyer suggest sending her to such a place?"

"On the grounds of her wealth, perhaps?" Mr Samuel suggests, pulling agitatedly at the floppy cravat at his neck to slacken it.

"She has nothing ... her house burnt down," I remind him.

"Yes, but the land it stood on will be worth something," says Mr Samuel. "And her deceased father no doubt left Miss Tulliver and her mother a reasonable allowance. If Mr Palmer-Reeves consigns Miss Tulliver to the lunatic asylum in Glasgow, then – as her guardian – he may have access to it all!"

Mr Samuel is now beside himself, quite sure of some dreadful plot.

"But the new Laird has inherited Tornish; Will has just told us of the plans he has to make himself quite rich from it," I say, trying to make sense of the awful suggestions Mr Samuel has put forward. "Why would he need Miss Tulliver's land and monies too?"

"Because rich folk are not like us," Will says fiercely. "They are never satisfied with their lot. They will never pass up an opportunity to get richer."

But I don't think Mr Samuel hears Will; he looks off across the bristling surface of the moor, his face lighting up as if he is a castaway on the ocean who has spotted land.

"Caroline!" he shouts, standing and waving as the girl all dressed in black comes running over the bumpy, coarse grasses, like a carefree child. And she runs unhindered, with her new-made veil unpinned and held carelessly in her hand.

"Hello!" she calls out giddily, almost lifting the spirits of this gloomy party.

"What are you doing here, my love?"

Mr Samuel says the last two words so easily, so naturally, that they almost go unnoticed.

Almost.

Effie and I exchange glances, then look to Miss Caroline. She is so pink-cheeked with the effort of running that it is impossible to tell if she blushes at those affectionate syllables. But her stumbling words show that she is taken aback.

"Oh! Oh, well … I … I have quite run away! Ha!" she laughs lightly. "But only for an hour or so. My guardian is newly ridden off to the furthest township, and Mrs Palmer-Reeves and Kitty are taking an afternoon nap."

And then her smile fades as she notices our downcast expressions.

"What is wrong? What has happened?" she asks, looking from one face to another.

My heart beats in my chest, waiting for Mr Samuel to tell her the awful truth he has guessed at. But before he can gather his words, her questioning gaze settles on Lachlan and the angry mark in plain sight on his cheek.

"Miss Kitty struck him," Effie says softly, her hand

moving our brother's flop of hair from his forehead.

"What? Oh, surely not! I cannot bear it. Lachlan, are you all right?" Miss Tulliver asks, dropping to her knees, the better to regard our brother.

Wearily, Lachlan props himself up, causing Miss Tulliver to gasp as she sees for herself the fiery, raised skin with bruises ripening. A tear trickles a zigzag route down Miss Tulliver's own marked cheek as she peels off a black glove and tenderly strokes her hand on Lachlan's downy skin.

"What is to be done…?" she says in a gentle but desperate voice.

As she speaks, I see Will's face darken and his jaw clench in a way that does not suit him, and puzzles me some. He is staring off towards the rocky outcrop that rises behind the pines. Perhaps he wishes he could scramble up there and roar his rage to the sky.

But I cannot think of that, not now Mr Samuel has done something so urgent and peculiar. For he has rushed over and dropped down by Miss Tulliver's side. Dropped down on one knee!

"I wish I had answers to all the wrongs that are happening here, but I do not," he says. "Though there is *one* thing I can do. One way to right one wrong. One way to help that would make me the happiest of men…"

What is happening here?

Is this a proposal?

Mr Samuel – does he mean to *wed* Miss Tulliver, to save her?

For if the "problem" of Miss Tulliver is solved this way, then the Laird will not have to consider his lawyer friend's outlandish notion of the asylum!

Effie suddenly sits up stiffly, her grey eyes widening as she too grasps Mr Samuel's meaning. I fancy we both hold our breath, awaiting Miss Tulliver's response.

"Samuel … I – I don't understand," she says, flopping back on the grass, as if she *does* understand but that the surprise of it has quite bowled her over.

Her suitor drops to the grass too, on both his knees and holding his hands together, as if to entreat Miss Tulliver of his earnest feelings.

"Hear me out, Caroline, I beg you," he begins. "If we had all the time in the world and you had a loving and dear family, then I would court you in the most steady and slow fashion. But we do not have all the time in the world, as I will leave for Glasgow next week. And more to the point, you do *not* have a loving and dear family, though no one deserves it more. And yes, I am much too lowly for you, dear, who should be the wife of some man of stature. But marry me, and I promise you will be my light and my love and my joy…"

Will, Lachlan, Effie and I – we are as still as the boulders on the nearby outcrop. The quiet stretches, the birdsong swells in the vacuum. But at last Miss Tulliver speaks.

"Yes, oh, *yes*, I will marry you!" she says in delight, though the water that runs from her eyes and even her nose could be mistaken for a sign of sadness by a stranger, instead of happiness and relief.

"Then it is settled!" Mr Samuel says in delight, reaching out to take Miss Tulliver's hands in his. "We will tell the Laird this day. He can have no objections, since he foolishly values you so little. Next week, we shall leave on the ferry together, and set off for my lodgings in Glasgow. Perhaps the old preacher can marry us here when he comes on Sunday, or we shall find someone to marry us when we get to the mainland. Even if we have to wait till we reach Glasgow, it will not matter. We will be together and…"

Mr Samuel's excited words fade to a babble in my mind, for I now see that Will is again staring, so intently now, at the top of the rocky outcrop. What can be so important as to take his attention from this glorious moment between our two friends?

Sensing something might be wrong, I look that way now, squinting my eyes against the sun. And now I see that there are three figures up there. Will's eyes are quite fixed upon them, and he seems uncommonly agitated.

"Excuse me, but there is something I must do," he suddenly says, and begins to hurry away, taking great strides around the little lochan that quickly turn into a run.

"Will?" I call after him. There is a tightness in my stomach that tells me something is far from well here. "I must see what the matter is…"

With that muttering to my sister and brother and the new sweethearts, I gather up my skirts and follow my friend.

"Will!" I shout, as he disappears into the dark-green shelter of the pines on the far side of the lochan. "Will, wait!"

It seems he does not wish to wait; as I dart beneath the cover of branches and leap over the tangle of roots, he shows me only his back, as if he wishes to be as far away from me as he can. But he cannot outrun me here; if we were on the flat moor he would win, but the uneven floor of the woods tricks him just as much as it does me. At last, as the effort of running burns my very lungs, I see Will take a wrong step and a tumble, just as the woods thin out and give way to the sunshine on the foot of the outcrop.

"For shame, Will!" I gasp, catching him up as he struggles to right himself. "What can be so terrible that you run from me so?"

"I am not running from you, Little Bird," he pants in answer. "I am running to stop *them*."

"Who? Who is up there?" I ask, glancing up at the

steep rocks. I know the other side to be steep too; the side that watches over the old droving road leading onward towards the most westerly township.

"My brother George, and Fergus and Donal," he says a little more steadily, as his breath calms. "They know the Laird has gone to see the last of his tenants today. They plan to lie in wait and attack him on his way back."

"Attack him?" I say, shock flooding my chest. "Do they mean to *kill* him?"

"No, no! They have a rope laid across the droving path, which they will pull up to make his horse fall," says Will, his eyes wide with the older boys' secret. "Before the Laird sees what is happening, they plan to come from behind and hit his skull with a stone, and then flee. They told me it would look like a rockfall has happened."

"But to what purpose?" I ask, despairing of this wild and wayward plan.

"They want him injured so that he may not be able to carry out his bad business. Or even so he gives up on the island and moves back to London."

"Will, this is *madness*!" I tell him with no uncertainty. "How could the lads be sure *that* would be the outcome? How could they be sure the Laird would not set eyes on them? And what is the difference between a blow that causes injury and one that kills a man – how can whichever one does the deed make his aim so fixed? Will, if they kill the Laird and are found out…"

"I know. It came to me now just how dangerous a task it is," Will says, getting back on his feet and beginning to clamber up the rocks. "And that's why I must stop them."

Of course I clamber quickly after my friend, faster than ever I have scaled the stones of the Glas Crags.

For perhaps George and the Matheson boys will listen to Will, and perhaps they will not. And if they do not, *I* can surely talk to them as the daughter of Robert MacKerrie, the most respected of the island's elders.

I know my father would tell them this is *not* the right action. I know he would counsel them to—

"NO!" Will shouts, as he reaches the summit a step or two before I do. But the sound of it is lost as a loud, chest-thumping crack rings out below.

Desperate to see what my friend is witnessing, I scramble closer, the loose covering of small stones underfoot making the going difficult.

As I struggle to steady myself, I glimpse the scene below … a horse tumbled to the ground, unable to right itself for the weight of the fallen rider – the Laird, holding firm to it. Another horse rearing, whinnying, as Mr Jenkins clutches its reins with one hand while something glints and smokes in his other.

"Stop, you cowards! I know who you are!" he roars,

red-faced, to the lads I cannot see from this vantage point, but who must now be fleeing.

A cold, hard sureness comes to me: the lawyer is holding a gun.

The panic of it makes me lose my balance completely on this unknown, uncertain surface, and I start slipping and sliding backwards on the shale.

"Little Bird!" I hear Will shout, as the ground seems to give way below me, sending me back down the way I came.

Twisted arms of gorse flash by, my desperate grasp missing them, my fingers instead tearing and bleeding on jagged stones.

And I begin to tumble now, over and over. Falling and falling and falling, like a bird shot on the moor...

Till my wing is pulled hard, and the shriek of searing pain gives way to sudden blackness.

CHAPTER 12

I am in Father's good chair, with the best cushions, right by the crackling fire.

He himself is not in need of it; he is gone to the Big House to try to plead for George, Fergus and Donal, or to find out what fate has befallen them.

And while we wait impatiently for news, I rest here with my head woozy from the warm milk and whisky Effie gave me for my pain ... though in truth, the shoulder of my weak arm still throbs maddeningly.

It came clean out of the socket when Will grabbed me on the outcrop and stopped me falling further. But once Mr Samuel carried me home, my sister expertly wrestled my shoulder till it cracked into position, afterwards binding it tight to me with a piece of cotton torn from the bottom of one of Miss Tulliver's petticoats.

Still, my wrenched arm is not what makes me so wretched.

"Shush now, Bridie," Effie says softly, from her seat at

the other side of the fire, where Lachlan sits curled at her feet like a sickly dog seeking solace from the warmth of the grate. "Is it paining you more?"

It is only on hearing my sister's kindly tone that I feel the fat, hot tears springing from my eyes.

"No, it is not that. I thought … I thought I might save the lads," I tell Effie haltingly, as the tears trip up my words. "Will did, too. But we failed!"

"You and Will did *not* fail, Bridie," Effie insists. "For did Will not save *you* this afternoon, and *you* him?"

I blink. Will did indeed save me from further harm, stopping me clattering on to the boulders that lay at the foot of the outcrop.

"But how did I save him?" I ask my sister.

"Bridie, he told me himself how he was frozen with fear, staring down for sightings of his brother or the other boys," Effie says earnestly. "It would have taken but a second for the Laird or his lawyer to glance up and see him – and suppose him to be part of the plot. In rushing to your rescue, you helped Will save himself. And we must be grateful for that."

Her words are balm to me indeed, more than any whisky and milk. Yet the gentleness and sense in them make we weep more, for she reminds me in this moment so much of Mother. Oh, how I miss—

The door is suddenly thrust open, and Father rushes in, his brown eyes as dark as pitch with rage, his breath ragged from hurrying to us.

"What is it? What has happened to George and the boys?" asks Effie, the colour quite lost from her face.

"It seems the three lads stole away to the cove and took Mr Matheson's rowboat," says Father, slamming the door shut behind him and scratching agitatedly at his beard. "We can only hope they are well on their way to the mainland by now."

"The mainland? But that is too far to go in just a rowing boat, is it not?" I say.

I know that the small boats are meant only for skirting around the island. To get to the mainland, folk wait for the ferry or hitch a lift on a fishing vessel.

"It *can* be done," says Father, with a hopeful light in his eyes. "If the lads aim for the rocky spit of land closest they can cut across the moors on foot to the town."

"Isn't there an old fellow that scratches a living from a croft somewhere out that way?" asks Effie. "Perhaps he might help them; give them a lift to town on his cart?"

"Mr Buchanan ... he keeps himself to himself, but he is a good man, and may well help the lads," Father replies. "I hope so; I hear one of the Laird's London men is readying to set sail for the town to get the law on them."

So Fergus and Donal will not be standing proud and handsome in their kilts by the harbour tomorrow morning, ready to play their fiddles after George pipes the Queen a welcome as her ship docks.

And more importantly, and sadder yet, the lads will never, ever again play those well-loved tunes and airs for the folk of Tornish...

"May they run so far and so fast that they are never found..." mutters Father, as if he is saying a prayer.

What he does *not* say is that we cannot contemplate another fate for them. Prison, or worse, is too desperate a thought.

"Does Ishbel know?" I ask, thinking of our sister, working hard at the Big House to prepare for the royal party, for the pittance she will – hopefully – be paid before she finds herself without work.

"Aye, and Mistress Matheson," Father says, nodding and staring down at the ground, as if it is hard to think of the despair of both his daughter and the Matheson brothers' mother.

"Father, could you not have asked the Laird to forgive George, Fergus and Donal?" Lachlan now asks, from where he is hunched on the floor and hugging on to Effie's skirts.

At that, Father gives a sigh that is more like a soft roar of despair, and clutches his head with both hands.

"Father?" I say urgently, knowing that there is something even *more* terrible that he must tell us.

"I did go to plead for the boys on behalf of their

families, though I knew it a fool's errand," he answers in a resigned voice. "What I did not suppose was that the Laird … that the Laird would blame *me* for the affair."

"You? But, Father, why would Mr Palmer-Reeves suppose that?" Effie asks, her grey eyes flashing with alarm.

"He supposes it because he and his crony came across me at the township he was visiting. *That* was enough to make him think that I plot and scheme with his tenants against him," Father tells us. "And with the Matheson lads and George caught trying to set upon him on his return, he is now certain that *I*, as the main elder, ordered them to do so."

"What does this mean, Father?" I ask, as a chill begins to replace the warm, woozy feeling inside me.

"It means that if he cannot have the lads punished," Father answers, "he will more than happily settle for me, I fear."

"No!" cries Effie with a voice sharp as a shard of glass. "Everyone on the island and beyond knows you to be honest and good!"

"But, Effie, not everyone is a rich and powerful laird," Father tells her, pounding one fist into the palm of the other hand, as if wishing he could do the same to Mr Palmer-Reeves. "And so – oh, forgive me, Bridget, my love! – we have no choice…"

"No choice but what?" I ask, scared now that he mentions Mother in such a grave tone.

"Your mother called us the lucky ones, to live our lives here on Tornish. But, my dears, our luck has run out. We must leave – all of us. Tomorrow," says Father, staring solemnly at us. "There is nothing for us here now."

"I knew it! There have been so many signs…" Effie wails, clutching her shawl tight around her.

I am not like my sister; I never was superstitious. But this morning at the Big House, I felt as if my family was undone and now I know it is so. And in the yawning silence after Father's declaration, I think each of our troubled minds turns to the one we leave behind, lying at her peace in the churchyard.

The one whose grave we will not be able to visit and place flowers on ever again, if we are to flee Tornish as Father insists…

"Listen, I have already spoken of this to Ishbel, and she will return home as soon as she is able," Father carries on, pausing only to comfortingly pat Effie on the shoulder and plant a tender kiss on her head. "Tonight, *now*, you must pack all that is most important, and carry it to our rowboat in the cove. And tomorrow morning, while the Queen lands on Tornish, we shall all be there to greet her at the harbour, as we should be."

"Father … I don't understand," whines Lachlan, looking so very alarmed.

"We will arouse no suspicion if we are seen to be there to welcome Her Majesty, my little lad," Father says to him, as he walks to the window and reaches for Mother's tin box hidden in the eaves above it. "And while everyone is quite distracted, we shall all quietly steal away."

"Where to?" asks Lachlan, as we watch Father take money from the box and stuff it in his pocket, before returning the tin to its hiding place.

"Glasgow, I think – it is a large place to hide away in, with good prospects for me to work," Father answers. "And I am away now to see John Mackay. I will pay him to take you and your sisters on board his fishing boat tomorrow, and away from here."

"Just us? Are you not coming on John's boat too, Father?" says Effie, alarmed.

"No, because I do not wish to have him accused of helping put danger his way," says Father, opening the cottage door. "If he is stopped with only you three girls and Lachlan on board, Ishbel is to say he is taking you to the mainland to visit family."

"And you will take the rowboat, Father?" I ask, picturing him crossing the choppy channel to the dangerous rocky outcrop he just spoke of.

"Yes, and I'll meet you on the outskirts of the town.

I built a barn for a farmer there two summers back – if you tell him you're my kin he'll let you hide away there till I can join you, I'm sure," Father explains. "And now I must go, there is much I need to arrange. And … and I'm sorry."

As the door closes on us, I feel too shocked to cry. But Effie and Lachlan give in to their tears and woe most mightily.

"Here," I tell them, struggling upright though all of my aches. "We must make haste. Lachlan, get the empty sacks from the byre. We can pack our things in those."

"But what should we take with us? What is important?" Effie cries in panic.

"Clothes, blankets, candles," I suggest, though I am not so certain myself. "Father's tools, some of the dried foodstuffs for our journey…"

I am as uncertain as my sister, but all I do know is that we can help Father by being as ready as we know how to be. Even if that means guessing.

And so two hours or more of effort passes, with things being packed and driven in the pony and cart to the rowboat, in readiness for our escape in the morning. (What will happen to our steady old pony once we are gone? What of the cows and the chickens and the good house that Father built for us? Oh, I mustn't think of that now…)

There is surely much more to be done, but I am a

poor help with my arm and tender bruisings. And Lachlan; Lachlan is grizzling, crazed with tiredness and worry, and so I shoo him to bed.

When I come back from settling him, I see my sister standing at the open door of the cottage, watching as the early summer evening light begins to fade outside. I pad across and stand alongside her, in time to see the rich glow of the sun as it dips down to the west. It is a sight we will not see again – from the sweet framing of this familiar doorway at least. Neither of us speaks, but I feel Effie's arm circle my waist, and I gratefully lay my head on her shoulder. I notice in this stillness that my secret self – the one who longs to leave – is lost for words for once, now that the harsh reality of our going looms large and heavy…

But my reverie is interrupted by a sudden yapping, and out of the gloaming, a light streak of dog comes loping towards us in a most odd fashion, followed by the hurrying figure of Ishbel, and one other. It is Mr Samuel!

He looks beside himself with grief. Does he know of our plans to leave undercover? I like Mr Samuel very much, but I do not think Ishbel knows him well enough to have trusted him with this sudden pressing secret of ours.

Then quick as a blink, a shared look passes between Ishbel, Effie and myself. I am certain of its meaning;

Mr Samuel knows nothing, and it is safest that way. The squeeze of a hand Ishbel gives us both as we all hurry inside tells us that we are together in what is to come. I have never felt so deep-down sure of my sisters and our bond. Mother would be proud!

"Listen, I cannot get sense out of him," Ishbel says to us in Gaelic as she throws off her shawl and Mr Samuel collapses on the settle. "I came across him and the dog in the woods on the way home. He was wailing as if the end of the world was come!"

"What of the dog?" asks Effie, as Patch tries to settle, with a limp and a whimper, by the fire.

"The Laird's mood is dreadful tonight," says Ishbel, quickly pouring water from the big black kettle into a cup for Mr Samuel. "He took out his rage on the pup with a well-placed kick of his boot, as he would. Here, give Mr Samuel this – if you are able."

Ishbel has been so rushed that she has only now seen my strapped-up arm, which Father must have told her of.

"Of course," I say, taking the tin cup from her with my good hand and carrying it over to Mr Samuel. I switch from Gaelic to English as I address him. "Sir, whatever can be the matter?"

"The Laird," says Mr Samuel, after pausing to take a deep breath and gather himself, "has refused his permission for Caroline and I to marry."

"You thought to *wed* Miss Tulliver?" Ishbel gasps, unaware of another of today's life-changing events.

"I did indeed, and Caroline was very happy to be my bride."

"It's true," Effie assures our incredulous older sister.

"What was the Laird's objection?" I ask Mr Samuel.

"He says the match is completely unsuitable," replies Mr Samuel, shaking his head as if he cannot believe what he must say next, "and that Caroline is not in her right mind to even consider it. In fact, he confidently and conveniently announced that he is so *sure* that she is not in her right mind, that he has decided to send her away … to the lunatic asylum in Glasgow."

Mr Samuel's despairing eyes meet mine, and I understand his pain. He had hoped his proposal would lessen the possibility of this threat. Instead he has played into Mr Palmer-Reeves' hands — it has given the Laird a solid reason to follow through with his lawyer's suggestion of ridding himself of his ward *and* gaining her fortune.

"Oh, my Lord, the poor girl," says a deeply concerned Ishbel, clutching at her chest. "What is to become of her?"

"What is to become of her indeed?" says Mr Samuel with an anguished shrug. "And what can I do to save her? As we speak, my things are being packed up. I am to be sent away tomorrow on a boat, before the Queen's arrival. I would insist Caroline comes with me, but no manservant of the Laird's is going to let that happen. Oh, my dear, sweet girl!"

He looks from one to the other of us beseechingly, but my sisters and I have no comforting words for him, though each one of us wishes she did, I am certain.

"Is your father here?" Mr Samuel says, sounding desperate and hopeful at the same time. "I know him to be an elder of the community and well respected, so perhaps he can somehow…"

Mr Samuel trails off, acutely aware that Father cannot, in truth, help in the situation – without realising what the truth of *our* desperate situation is.

Maybe it is because my senses are raw and my body is sore, but I suddenly find myself yearning for someone whose soothing words and gentle hand could always ease the stings and hurts of childhood…

And then I wonder if my sisters are of that same mind in that moment too. The three of us; we look at each other in slow and steady understanding. An understanding of what our mother would say, what she would want us to do. Our luck has run out, and so has Miss Tulliver's. If we are to flee, then so must she.

"Mother would not want a girl left alone to such a wolf," says Ishbel in Gaelic. "We have to do something."

Mr Samuel, understanding nothing of what's just

been said, watches as Effie and I nod in reply to Ishbel's words.

And I feel comforted to know that while we must leave Mother behind, Mother will never truly leave my sisters and I.

CHAPTER 13

It is near time.

I stand statue-still in the watching crowd as the royal steamship chugs ever closer.

"I cannot see Her Majesty yet!" says Lachlan, standing on his toes and peering at the faint dark dots of heads looking our way from the ship's deck. Which one of them will become the grave face of the small Queen it is hard to tell, and I don't suppose Lachlan, Effie and I will find out.

Our purpose was to be seen to be here, among the folk gathered by the harbour – just as Ishbel is at her post in the kitchen at the Big House – so that Mr Palmer-Reeves would not anticipate Father's plans for our family to flee.

Everyone in the crowd knows it, of course.

Our fellow islanders might be listening and nodding along as Father plays the bagpipes – stepping in for the departed George – but they are all ready to shuffle together and close the circle when the fiddlers take over and we quietly slip away, one by one.

"Do you think the Queen passed by Mr Samuel out on the water?" Lachlan asks now.

"Shush," hisses Effie, as if the mention of the painter will bring us bad luck.

"Perhaps," I answer more steadily. And perhaps Mr Samuel, laden with his equipment, will indeed have caught sight of the royals as he was ushered away from Tornish in disgrace earlier this morning, sailed to the town on the mainland in the Laird's own boat.

At that thought, I turn from the view of the ship to the sight of Mr Palmer-Reeves. He stands nearby, along with his wife, haughty daughter and the loathsome Mr Jenkins, all preening like proud peacocks.

But wait – something appears to be amiss with Miss Kitty; her cheeks are flushed a fierce pink in her pale-powdered face and her bosom heaves in her cream lace dress.

"What is wrong with her?" I whisper to Effie, with a slight nod to indicate who it is I speak of. "It looks as if she cannot catch her breath…"

"Vanity, I would guess," Effie says with disdain in her voice. "She must have got her maid to tie her corset too tight!"

I think my sister must be right. Miss Kitty's waist this day is *so* very tiny – it looks as if a pair of hands might encircle it with ease. It is so very small in fact that if a brisk wind blew up off the sea and bent her backwards she might snap clean in half.

A tug at my arm pulls me from that pleasant thought.

"Should I go now?" Lachlan whispers to myself and Effie.

I glance over at Father, at the other side of the harbour from us, where he stands with his pipes, ringed by the other musicians.

My glance is a question – the nod he gives me as he plays is my answer.

"Yes," I tell our brother. "See you in a few minutes. Go!"

"Bless him," I hear Mistress Beaton say beside me, as she moves aside to let Lachlan slip away, then steps back into her place.

If it would not draw attention, I would hug her, for the pain and worry she must suffer over the disappearance of her George, *and* for allowing her remaining son to help us. Will is somewhere in another part of the waiting crowd now, but he too will move off soon; our pony and cart is tied up not far away – a tarpaulin covering the sacks packed with our few things – and Will is set to take us all to the bay by his township, where John Mackay's fishing boat is moored, waiting for this day's strange cargo.

"I'm away now," Effie murmurs in my ear, and I dare not look around at her, but hope my sister sees my nod as she lets herself be swallowed into the background.

A moment more, and I shall do the same.

And in that moment, I allow myself a small smile; Mr Palmer-Reeves does not know it, but he has done us a good service – by demanding nearly all his staff as well as tenants to be here, and by confining Miss Tulliver to her room for the duration of the Queen's visit, he has unwittingly allowed her escape!

While we stand here, Ishbel will have slipped out of the kitchens of the Big House, with Miss Tulliver by her side, smuggled out from under the noses of the one or two London staff left behind to ready the dining room for the royal visit. But they would not recognise the Black Crow anyway, not in the ordinary bundle of Mother's clothes that Ishbel brought for her to wear. If they glanced up from their polishing and perfecting, they would surely think her a washerwoman or at least some other person of no consequence.

A small, sparkling, chinking sound and a murmur of voices interrupts my reverie.

The children in front of me step aside as a fine-cut glass vial rolls by their bare feet, gently clunking to a stop by my own uncomfortable, Sunday-best black boots.

"Quick, grab it up! Bring it here!" Mistress Palmer-Reeves urges me, and I see that Miss Kitty is swaying, eyes fluttering, propped up by the sullen maid Maude, who is currently all aflap at the swoon the young lady finds herself in.

And so what am I to do but pick up the stoppered bottle, uncertain what it might contain, and take it over as I am bid?

"Open it up, girl, and let Kitty breathe in the smelling salts!" the Mistress demands of me.

I do not know what smelling salts are, but as soon as I take the stopper out, I am quite overcome by the stench – like days'-old pee in a chamberpot! And once I steady myself, it gives me the greatest of pleasure to waft the bottle and its sharp, foul odour under Miss Kitty's prim nose.

It is no surprise that the Laird's daughter rallies, squirming in Maude's grasp, her yellow-lashed eyes fluttering.

"What? Who?" she babbles, as she takes gulps of air, and tries to push the bottle away with her soft-gloved hand.

"You had a little turn, darling," her mother says distractedly, as she waves at one of the London servants, who quickly scurries over, unfolding a small wooden folding chair as he runs. "You will be quite well again shortly."

In fact, Miss Kitty is well enough to open her eyes now and see who is before her.

"Argh! Get that ugly thing away from me!" she yelps, suddenly smacking my weaker hand away, as if it were some creature's claw that she has beheld. A kick from her pretty pointed shoe cracks my shin at the same time. "Get out of my sight!"

Perhaps the jarring pain in both my shoulder and leg get the better of me.

Whatever the cause, I look that spoiled, nasty girl in the face and whisper, "I go with pleasure, miss. And I will be glad *never* to be in your company again."

Miss Kitty's pale eyes narrow, as I thrust the splashing vial of stinking stuff into her maid's chubby hand.

Hurrying back to the crowd, I risk a glance at Father, and see the frown of worry on his face; worry at what I may have just said, worry that I should be gone by now.

Slipping by Mistress Beaton, I am glad my sisters and I have spared Father one *more* worry … for he has no clue that my sisters and I have decided to help Miss Tulliver escape with us.

The truth is, last night we decided *not* to tell Father, lest he forbade it. We had no doubt of his railing against the terrible injustice that was to be done to Miss Tulliver, but we *also* knew he would fret that helping her escape from the island would put all of *us* in danger. When Father finally returned home last night, he was troubled enough on seeing the Laird's injured dog settled by our fire. All he knew of *that* was the creature had followed Ishbel home from work, as she had told it, missing out the fact that Mr Samuel had been here. So yes, we understood the worries Father would have concerning the possible rescue of Miss Tulliver, but we chose to … to think like Mother, I suppose.

A girl was in trouble and that just could not be overlooked.

"Take care, Bridie," whispers Mistress Beaton, before giving a cheer, which is taken up by all the people. And the rousing cries for the approaching Queen, accompanied by the song of the pipes, means I can vanish, quite unnoticed.

Hauling up my skirts, I take flight, hurrying along the dirt track inland, passing Will's steady horse that is tied to a tree, my heart singing when I see that my friend has beaten me to it and is already at my own father's pony and cart.

"Does danger make you smile, then?" he teases me, as I leap up beside him.

I cannot tell my friend that now our scheme begins in earnest, my secret self is bursting with the thrill of seeing the world beyond Tornish. I might have always fancied myself travelling west, but south-east – to Glasgow – is adventure enough.

"I smile at the sight of *you*, Will Beaton!" I jest with him instead – then see that he is not giving me his gap-toothed grin in reply.

"Well, you won't smile when you hear what I have to say," he says, shaking the reins to speed the pony on.

"What is it?" I ask, as I spy the yawning arms of the churchyard yew tree up ahead, and the figures of my two sisters, Miss Tulliver and my brother sheltering in its safe shadow. In Lachlan's arms, there is a wriggling bundle: on our way to the harbour, Lachlan stopped and tied Patch up at the back of the church, till we could come fetch him.

"I had quick words with John Mackay's wife back at the harbour," Will says, "and she tells me John is very vexed. Only an hour since, he talked to her of the risks of being caught with you three girls and Lachlan."

"But he will still take us?" I ask, flutters of fear in my stomach as I study the four nervously hopeful faces of the group we approach.

"I am sure that he is so very close to abandoning this plan that you must get on board as quick as you can, before he changes his mind. And I tell you now, he will not take the Laird's dog, never mind a lass he is guardian to!"

Chilled by Will's words, I shakily hold tight as he draws the cart to a shuddering halt.

"Quick!" he says, holding a hand out to help Miss Tulliver up, as my sisters and brother confidently clamber on to the flat bed of the cart.

"I must thank you and your sisters so much for helping me, Little Bird!" Miss Tulliver says, smiling sweetly at me as the cart lurches off, and she struggles to hold on to a large bag she has brought with her, and the rough shawl that is slipping from around her head.

The flutters in my stomach are replaced by a curdling in the pit of it as I look at Miss Tulliver's trusting face. I had meant to stop awhile at Mother's grave, but now I think she would agree there is no time to spend on the dead – only the living.

But how can I bear to tell Miss Tulliver that she will not be reunited with her beloved Mr Samuel at the harbour on the mainland soon enough?

How can I be so close to saving Miss Tulliver from the asylum in Glasgow, and fail now?

The answer is, I cannot.

I must not.

I *will* not.

Patting Miss Tulliver's hand, I stay silent, and let a plan come to me while the minutes pass and we jiggle and rattle and speed towards Will's township.

And as a fork in the track approaches – left heading for the township, right for the little cove where Father's rowboat sits ready – I have it.

"Stop!" I call out, and pull at the reins in Will's hands.

"What is it?" asks Ishbel, glancing around to see if something is amiss.

"Will tells me John Mackay expects the three MacKerrie sisters and their wee brother, and no one else," I say to my frowning sisters and Will. "And *that* is who will come on board his boat. At least, that is who he will *think* it is."

"Bridie! What nonsense are you intending?" Ishbel demands, as Miss Tulliver, Effie and Lachlan look on aghast.

But I am already taking my leave, grabbing Patch from my startled brother as I jump down from the cart.

"It is quite simple – the pup and I will go with Father in the rowboat," I say, sounding braver than I feel, when I think how far the little boat must travel to reach the safety of the ragged finger of rock Father is aiming for. "Miss Tulliver, when you get to John's fishing boat, you must hide your face – pretend to cry, perhaps – so he will not know you from me. And stoop in your sadness, so John does not notice that you are taller than I!"

"No, no!" Miss Tulliver says, and goes to clamber from the cart. "It should be *me* that goes with your father!"

At her words, I see that Ishbel and Effie understand that my plan is the only one that will work; Father will not expect Miss Tulliver to be waiting in the cove for him. And so they gently hold her back as I hurry away.

"No, Bridie is right; she the lightest for the rowboat," I hear Effie explain to her.

"*Beannachd agus deagh fhortan!*" I call out my goodbyes and good luck in Gaelic as cheerfully as I can. "See you over on the mainland!"

And with that, I set the dog down on the dusty, stone-scattered track, and holding him by the rope around his neck I begin to run in earnest, which is harder than I imagined, with the ache from my strained shoulder.

"Hey!" I hear Will's voice call out, and find him running after me.

"What are you doing?" I ask, as he draws level with me.

"Your sister Effie is every bit as good at driving the pony as I am," says Will, "so I passed her the reins, and will keep you company until your father gets to the cove."

And his smile, with those bright eyes and the gap where a tooth should be sends the flutters and curdles clean away, replacing them with a feeling like ... like sunshine.

So together we run, my oldest friend and I, and soon we are at the cove, where the tethered rowboats of the villagers bob at the shoreline.

I slow down, flopping on to the beach so that I might take my hated boots off. I'll need my feet bare and my skirts tucked in to push our boat into deeper water. Father will not be long – he is to ride Will's own waiting pony, and it's a sprightly young thing.

As I pull at the laces and wriggle the boots off, my secret self begins to sing out again, and I feel like I can hold the voice in no longer.

"Will, can I tell you of a dream I often have?" I ask

him, as he begins to untie Father's boat in readiness.

"Aye," he says, gazing back at me as his fingers expertly work at the damp rope, though he is hampered more than a little by Patch, who thinks it a game.

"Sometimes I dream that I am on top of the Glas Crags," I tell him as I stand, putting my boots around my neck with the laces I have tied together.

"With me?" he asks, as I walk towards him, rolling and tucking my skirts in.

"Not with you, no; I am quite alone," I say, feeling the cold slap of the water on my legs and bending to push the boat, as Will is doing. "And then a wind comes, and carries me clean away from Tornish!"

"My, that is a sad dream to have, Bridie MacKerrie!" he announces, holding the boat steady enough in the deeper water that I might scramble in.

"No, it is a joyful one to me, Will Beaton," I counter, feeling clumsy as a newborn calf as I haul myself aboard.

"Well … if we are telling each other secrets, then I too have always had a dream, Little Bird," my friend replies. "But it is very different to yours. And you appear most clearly in mine."

Our eyes meet, and there is such a tenderness in his expression that I find myself suddenly shy of his meaning. But only shy, not angry as I might have been in the past.

Before Will can say more that might make me shyer

still, my father thunders into the cove on Will's foaming-mouthed pony.

He may be surprised to see us here, but there is something more desperate on his mind than to go asking for our reasons.

"I think I hear a horse and rider coming after me!" he calls out, jumping from his steed. "Someone must have seen me go."

Father immediately splashes and wades into the waves, while the pony prances on the sand, uncertain what to do.

The curdling in my stomach returns, and I think of my words to Miss Kitty – how I would be glad never to see her again – and remember that her pale eyes studied me in that moment, as if she were puzzling over my words. Did she suspect? Did she mention something to her parents, who watched for Father leaving?

Oh, we are in danger of being discovered – and it is all the fault of my hot temper!

Still, there is nothing I can do but make haste.

"Pass him up!" I say to Will, who is already scooping the paddling Patch from the water.

The little boat lurches madly as he hands the dog into my arms, what with Father clambering on board beside me.

"Get yourself out of here, Will," Father says urgently. "Ride away along the shoreline and you'll soon be out of sight of anyone coming."

"Yes, sir," Will says, then stares at me with an intensity I am not used to. "Oh, Little Bird – *A h-uile latha sona dhut, 's gun latha idir dona dhut.*"

"*May every day be happy for you, and no day ever bad…*"

I cannot answer him.

I cannot speak.

That old Gaelic saying, one laden with sweet affection, has quite unravelled me, and all I can do is watch – blinking hard – as Will turns his attention back to the stern of the boat.

Making a sound between a groan and a roar, he gives one last hard shove against the tide to send us on our way.

His effort works; we lurch further out, now sucked by the cresting waves, Father splashing his oars into the choppy water.

"Will!" I call out to the boy who stands waist-deep in the buffeting sea, watching me go from him. "Will!"

"Leave! HURRY!" Father shouts at him.

At last I see that Will does as he is bid, and lopes dripping out of the sea, beckoning his horse over to him and quickly mounting it before galloping off along the shoreline.

I turn on my wooden plank of a seat, so that I might watch my dear friend become smaller, borne quite away from me … all the time unsure if the salt taste in my mouth is sea spray or the tears that are streaming down my face.

This far out, the waves are smaller, and I risk rising a little from my perch for one last glimpse before I lose sight of my Will altogether.

"Just in time," Father says to me, sounding alarmed. "There's someone at the cove now! Is it that Jenkins man?"

The familiar crack startles me – and I know that Father is right.

"Good God, is he *shooting* at us? Hold on, Bridie, hold on!"

But I am not holding on.

I am still half risen, and with the shock of the gunshot coupled with the sudden, barging surge of a wave, I am flung from the boat in the blink of an eye.

There is a moment … a fleeting moment when I turn and twist in the weightless air – and then I crash hard into the cold of the endless ocean, where the weight of my dress and the boots I have draped around my neck act like stones to sink me.

And – oh! – under the waves, the strangeness is the quiet. My limbs might struggle, but it is a soundless struggle as the sea blocks up my ears, and tries to force itself into my mouth. As if the sea itself wants to show this little bird that it is stronger than the sky she stares up into so often, so longingly.

Or is the island playing a joke on me, *punishing* me, for wanting to flee it so badly?

Tornish, or maybe all its magic sprites and such that I refused to believe in, have decided that I may never leave. Perhaps my destiny is to be found, washed up on the shore, with seaweed as my shroud, and be buried next to Mother in the churchyard.

Mother.

At the thought of her, a surge fills my heart.

An undertow sweeps warm below me, lifting me, I rise higher, my bulging eyes fixed on a shape above.

A final, silken lift and I am risen enough – enough for Father's muscled arm to wrap around me and I am scooped up like a stray pearl from the seabed.

As Father heaves and drags me back on board, I can just make out that we are drifted far enough from shore that no bullet can touch us.

"Bridie! Bridie!" Father sobs, clutching me to him as the little dog huddles shivering into my side. "I thought you were lost!"

But I am not lost, I realise, as I flop weakly into his embrace and stare back at Tornish, at the looming mass of the Glas Crags.

I might not know where we are bound, but I am on the journey I was meant to take.

And I will never be lost from my family on the way, not if I trust the guiding hand of she who is always in my heart, who will always remind me that I am luckier than many Highland girls that came before me.

She who gave birth in a storm but trusted what the old Laird said: that one day, her broken little bird would fly.

THE CITY
OF GLASGOW,
1862

CHAPTER 14

I do not dream any more.

Well, I have no dreams that are vivid and clear enough to stay in my mind, not once slivers of light come to wake me through the small window of the attic room in Glasgow that I share with my sisters.

I do see ghosts, though; *all* we girls do. Effie will go to the market for her mistress, and drop her basket when she sees a maid that looks like the sulky Maude. Ishbel says her blood runs cold if she strolls along Sauchiehall Street with Caroline and spies some dainty fool's umbrella bobbing along. Myself, I'll jump at the sound of a banged door, and think it Mr Jenkins setting off his gun once again. And Caroline – in her lawyer's office to sign the papers that would grant her independence from her guardian – nearly fainted when a moustachioed man barged in … but he was only another client, in the wrong office.

Of course, we all know our ghosts are that: twisted memories that will stop haunting us – one day.

LITTLE BIRD FLIES

But what I do have that is dear to me is my new hill.

It is not nearly so high and rocky and dramatic as the Glas Crags, which I last saw blearily, after my unexpected dip in the sea last summer. (I was sure then that I saw Will waving at me from the top, but Father and I were rowed so far away, so close to the rock-laced edges of the mainland, it might just have been the wings of a swooping sea eagle.)

From up here, on my new hill, the views are not of the rolling Atlantic Ocean, scattered islands rising from its depths, or the distant, snow-peaked mountains of the mainland.

Instead, I have found myself a long, low rolling hillock, I suppose, and the views I see from my new vantage point – of jumbled, jagged rooftops, spires and chimneys; the bustle of boats on the brown River Clyde – are staggering and wondrous in their own way. More importantly, for the last year, it is where I have come to speak to Mother.

"There," I say, placing the posy of wild violets at the feet of the stone angel, which sits on top of a solid white column of headstone. At my own feet, Patch is turning in circles, ready to settle himself down for a welcome rest after the walk here. He is only small, and his limp seems to tire him. Unlike me: I can still walk for miles, though these days I trample over pavement and cobbled road instead of cool grass and rough stone. It is made

easier for me now that I have soft boots that fit: a gift –
one of many to myself and my family – from Caroline.

"I don't know why you do that," Lachlan says
sulkily, kicking a stone that clips and skitters down the
slope, bouncing off so many people's graves as it goes,
disturbing their endless sleep. "It is not even *her*."

Of course I know this grave is not Mother's. The name
so neatly carved upon it is not "Bridget MacKerrie"; it
is "Eliza Garnett". She was the wife of a sea captain,
the words tell me. A loving wife and mother. Taken too
soon.

The vast Necropolis Cemetery is a picturesque and
peaceful place, as Samuel described it to me some long-
ago day in Tornish. Its avenues of trees and planting
making it as much a favourite of the folk of Glasgow
to walk around as any park or gardens. But when I first
visited with Samuel and Caroline – who will not have
us call them "Mr" or "Miss" or "Mistress" as we are such
good friends – I found myself drawn to this particular
monument.

Perhaps it was because its occupant, Eliza, was thirty-
seven years old, the same age as Mother when she was
struck down. Or perhaps it was because Eliza's angel
seemed to look down on me gently with blank, smooth
eyes. I felt soothed by that calm gaze. And it was, after
all, a time when I needed soothing…

You see, I had been a fool. Before we fled to the city,

LITTLE BIRD FLIES

I was secretly sure that of *all* my family, the shock of Glasgow would trouble me the least. What conceit!

How was it possible to arrive in a city that is as big as the whole of Tornish, but entirely covered in more streets and buildings than you could ever fathom, and not feel frightened? And how could you not be deafened by the constant din of lumbering carriages rattling over cobbles, or the clatter and banging from every direction, as great buildings go up and railway cuts go down? How could you not wince at the odours that assault you, from the cloying smoke that churns from the forest of tall factory chimneys, the stench from the chemical and dye works, the terrible reek – like a byre that is never cleared nor cleaned – from the Wynds where the poorest sort are unfortunate enough to live?

I *did* settle, in time, of course. But still it makes me shudder to think that – like so many displaced Highlanders – *we* might have ended up in the Wynds too, in one of those dank, mean lanes with their tall, thin, crumbling houses packed with families in each festering room.

We were lucky; with the money in Mother's tin box (bolstered by the islanders who bought the goods and beasts we left behind on Tornish), we had enough for the rent on a little better of a place. Father's skills also meant he soon got work, thankfully. And our luck also came in the form of Samuel and Caroline... Naturally, Father was shocked when he discovered the secret rescue of Caroline that Ishbel, Effie and myself had undertaken. But with the deed done – and my own more recent rescue from the sea itself – Father quickly forgave us, and set his mind more to getting us as far from Tornish and trouble as he could. Reunited, Caroline and Samuel had set off ahead of us, taking the fastest stagecoach they could afford so that they might get quickly to Glasgow and be married for decency and safety's sake. Once we arrived after our slower route – past the farms and places Father had worked in, where he could call on favours of food and a cart ride to the next town – Samuel looked around for decent lodgings for us. "It was the least I could do," he told Father, when he took us, all tired and bedraggled from our journeying, to some rooms above a little shop where he bought his art supplies.

I am ashamed to say my heart sank when I went up the creaking back stairs and found our new home to be two dark, cold, comfortless little attic rooms, with nothing but a bed in each and a blackened fire and range in the bigger of the two.

"There is a market, not too far, that sells all manner of good-quality second-hand furnishings," Samuel had said quickly, apologetically. "We would have picked you some things ourselves, if we had more time."

"It will do us fine," Father had assured him, while Caroline looked in vain for somewhere to lay down the basket of food she had brought us as a welcoming gift.

And our new home, naturally, *is* fine. With a dresser, tables, chairs and rugs bought, the rooms have long since taken on a less despairing air. Our few beloved things from Tornish were placed around by Ishbel and Effie and I; a lace cloth here, an embroidered cushion there; the china dogs and clock on the mantle, pictures on the wall – including the now-framed drawing Samuel made of we three sisters by the fire in the cottage the day Mistress Palmer-Reeves came to visit.

The important thing is, it is truly a cosy home that Father, Ishbel and Effie love to come back to after a day's work.

And now that schooling is finished for the summer, our home is my domain entirely; while Father labours at Broomielaw Quay, Ishbel keeps house for Samuel and Caroline, and Effie is a maid in a villa nearby, *my* work is to stay home and cook and clean and look after Lachlan.

The first two I do with no complaint, for who else would take care of these duties, while my sisters are earning decent money for the family?

The third is a more difficult task. My nine-year-old brother does not *want* to be looked after. Especially since I have stayed small and slight, while he is sprouting and already a little taller than me!

"I'm away," he says curtly to me now, hunching his shoulders against any argument.

"But we are expected at Mrs Lennox's house shortly!" I remind him, to no effect, as he has already broken into a sprint and is determined not to heed my words. In fact, my words are drowned out by his whistling for Patch, who leaps up and quickly limps after his beloved companion.

"I do not know what to make of him," I lean back on the stone and tell Mother, as I watch Lachlan disappear behind the shelter of headstones and trees, with Patch barking and chasing behind. "He is so very changed from the lad he was on Tornish! I wonder if he too sees ghosts but will not admit to being feared by them…"

Certainly, where Lachlan was once sweet, he is now sullen. Once he was my shadow and I was so sure of his adoration; now he cannot be doing with me, preferring the company of Alec, a boy from school he has been running with these last months. I would be glad that Lachlan at last has a friend his age, but I am not taken with this Alec. I came home not so long ago, laden with stuff for our supper, only to find this dark-haired, elfin-like lad in the kitchen with Lachlan. He looked at me most insolently, with a mocking smile on his face when he saw me walk in my usual halting way.

"But do not worry, I will *always* my keep my patience with Lachlan and I will *always* protect him," I say, giving Mother a solemn promise, even though the patience part is sometimes difficult indeed…

LITTLE BIRD FLIES

In the distance, a church bell tolls, alerting me to the time and the fact that Mrs Lennox is expecting her visitors, though she will have to make do with just me.

"Goodbye, Mother," I tell her, pressing my fingers first to my lips then to Eliza's gravestone.

With that kiss to my dearest kin, I take my leave of the angel and meander down the path between the headstones, glancing up as I go at the plump grey pigeons that flap above me. They may not have the white beauty of the seagulls of home, or the majesty of the giant sea eagles that glide around the tip of the Crags, but they have a sound so pleasing and comical that it always makes me smile.

And one year on, I listen for every sound this teeming city has to offer.

For the more I hear of the world around me, the less I am afraid of the ghosts of the past or the wily whispers of my secret self.

CHAPTER 15

"OOO-oh-OOO-oh-EH!"

What must passers-by think of this scrawny girl making such a strange noise as she ambles along?

I don't much care, of course. Folk can think what they want of me humming my daft tune all the way to Mrs Lennox's, the cooing sound of it to mimic the city birds, and the rhythm of it a likeness of the milking songs of home.

Before I know it, I find myself at a neat, green, square of a park, with four roads leading off it, all of them containing rows and rows of grand red sandstone villas. I turn into the first road I come to and am quickly at Mrs Lennox's gate. Her garden is filled with bonnie shrubs and rose bushes and I take a deep breath of them as I pass the imposing front door, glistening with a glossy dark-blue paint and shining brass knob, with a matching circular knocker.

Of course, I would not dream of touching the door knocker, unless – like Effie – I was tasked to polish it. For the side entrance is where I am headed, as I often am if I stop by to wait for Effie to finish up her work. Though today is different, I suppose … rather than sitting at the kitchen table – where I have met Mrs Lennox many times when she has come to discuss household issues with Effie – I am instead invited for afternoon tea, in the main house, no less!

"Come away in!" Effie calls out from the kitchen, when she spies me through the door she has left open for me, or for *us*, rather. "Where's Lachlan?"

"He would not come; he bolted from me," I tell her.

In the old days on the island, Effie's mood would have darkened at that, and I would have expected the sharp edge of her tongue. But since we came here, since we worked together to flee the island, she treats me – thankfully – as her equal.

"Oh, that lad wearies me, he really does," Effie sighs, as she busies herself setting a china tea service on a big silver tray. "Still, you are here, Bridie. Come on, follow me through…"

My heart gives such a lurch of excitement as I trot after my sister, watching her stiff grey poplin skirt flounce as she walks. Effie's pretty plumpness is pinched into an hourglass waist that she is *so* proud of, even if she does sigh and grumble fastening herself into her corset in the mornings. She is also very taken with the dainty, lace-edged muslin cap tied about her dark-red hair, one of several given to her by her mistress.

"Ah, now, here she is!" calls out Mrs Lennox, as I timidly walk behind Effie into the drawing room. "The lovely Bridie!"

Here in Glasgow, there is no one to call me Little Bird. Even Samuel and Caroline – who old Mrs Lennox knows through their mutual charitable work – have slipped into using my given name, though I never asked them to. It is as if my pet name has been left behind on Tornish, along with dear Will. But I barely register what Mrs Lennox calls me at all; I am too in awe of the room I find myself in. I thought the apartments of Samuel and Caroline to be beautiful, full of lovely furnishings and rich colour, especially the light-filled room that is Samuel's painting studio, but this splendour is something that my eyes struggle to take in.

It has been that way so often since I came to Glasgow, of course. I am constantly boggling at the intricate decoration on the five-storey buildings on the main streets, or the arching span of the bridges over the Clyde. I cannot take my gaze away from the trains I have seen growling into the cavernous station. I have stared at the stately statue of Queen Victoria on its imposing plinth in George Square, wishing I might have seen such a regal, if small, person in the flesh, had circumstances been different.

And this room also is a wonder in itself. Lusciously

thick curtains drape like velvet waterfalls to the polished floor, which is covered by a carpet of a most fascinating pattern. (For a moment, I wish I was my barefoot self again, so I could feel the softness of the wool between my toes…)

Everywhere I look, there are padded and cushioned chairs, and tables – so many elegantly spindly, small tables – decked with ornate knick-knacks and plants in pots. Strange-leafed plants that surely *must* originate from some faraway place, like a jungle in the Amazon, I should think! The walls too heave with thick-framed pictures and paintings and mirrors and gas-light sconces.

"Bridie?" Ishbel remonstrates gently, widening her eyes at me from her position on a sofa next to Caroline.

I realise that my mouth is hanging open in surprise and that I have entirely forgotten my manners.

"Good afternoon, Mrs Lennox," I say politely, giving the effortlessly elegant old lady a little bob. "I'm sorry it's only myself here. My brother could not come, I'm afraid."

"Ah, that's a shame … I would have liked to meet him," Mrs Lennox says with a friendly smile, and a hand that ushers me to sit down. "I'm sure he's as delightful as his three sisters."

As I settle into the nearest chair, I exchange the smallest of knowing glances with Effie as she sets the tray down, and do the same with our elder sister. "Delightful" is perhaps not the most appropriate description of Lachlan these days, we all know. He is no longer a shy pup, but now roams the streets like a cocky stray.

But – ha! – now I see a hint of a smile playing at Ishbel's lips at this same thought, and I must struggle not to laugh out loud! How wonderful it is to see Ishbel so changed from the serious, gaunt girl she was. Working for Samuel and Caroline, where she is considered more companion than housekeeper, has lifted the mantle of sternness she always wore back in Tornish.

"Bridie, Mrs Lennox has had the most wonderful idea, and she needs your help," says Caroline, gazing at me with excited anticipation from her place beside Ishbel.

She too is so very changed. Long gone is her garb of the Black Crow. Now Caroline wears pretty dresses of patterned poplin in the liveliest of spring colours. And each one is matched with an elegant hat, which is always styled with a soft, net veil. It is cover enough that strangers passing in the street will not see the detail of Caroline's face and stare, but for those whom she talks with, the marks she bears are quite clear to see – and she has no trouble with that at all. Caroline's new confidence, I think, comes from being painted and drawn endlessly by her adoring young husband.

"Quite!" Mrs Lennox bursts out in agreement with Caroline, rousing me from my momentary wistfulness.

"Now, Bridie, you are aware of the cause closest to my heart?"

"Yes," I said with a nod, neatly resting my hands together in my lap and trying my best not to wriggle with excitement at the strangeness of being in such a grand room, in such grown-up company.

I do indeed know the cause closest to Mrs Lennox's heart. As with Caroline, she despairs of the slum conditions so many people of Glasgow live in. Caroline has spoken of the many years Mrs Lennox has supported the prominent folk of the city who campaign for better sanitation, education and welfare for the unfortunate inhabitants of the Wynds and beyond, especially the children, who often work from tender years in the factories of the ever-growing city.

But what troubles Mrs Lennox the most is the scourge of alcohol. "Life is so terrible, it is no wonder that the fathers, and sometimes mothers, drown their sorrows in drink," Caroline once told me earnestly. "But Mrs Lennox says that money wasted on drink sees food taken from the very mouths of babes!"

And so Caroline and Mrs Lennox are in a society called the Temperance Movement. They hold rallies and talks with banners and bugles, all in an attempt to get those who rely on alcohol to see the error of their ways.

"Well, I have come up with an excellent scheme," says Mrs Lennox, her eyes shining. "We in the Movement have aimed our words at the men and the women who frequent public houses. But now we have decided on a different path. Next week, we will hold a fair in the garden square by the church."

"Like Glasgow Fair?" I ask, talking of the yearly stalls and entertainments that appear on the Green every summer. We arrived just after it last year, but I hope Father permits us to attend this *next* fair, for it is surely a sight to see, with bands playing and wild animals on show and fire-breathers too, I hear tell!

"It will be a smaller affair entirely, and will be *just* for children," Mrs Lennox explains. "We want to attract as many vulnerable little ones from the Wynds as possible. After some traditional entertainments, there will be a marionette show, which will be amusing and diverting, yet educate them about the perils of drink."

"Yes, because if we cannot reach the parents, we can reach the next generation, Mrs Lennox hopes!" adds Caroline, as she takes one of the cups and saucers that Effie is handing out.

A marionette show … oh, I should like to see that too! It is dolls, or puppets, made to move and talk and dance by wires on a perfect little stage of their own. But still; what do Mrs Lennox's plans have to do with me being invited here for afternoon tea?

"Bridie, I have had these handbills printed," says Mrs Lennox, holding up a colourful piece of paper that advertises the fair. "And I was hoping that I could engage your services, and that of your brother, to hand these out to the children you think at risk. You and Lachlan are so much closer to their age; they may respond better than if some silly old person such as myself tries to badger them to come. And I would pay you both for your time, naturally."

"Why, yes … yes, I'd like to help," I say, taking a cup and saucer into my own hand.

I am quite taken with the idea of helping Mrs Lennox, not just because it is a good-hearted and well-intentioned notion, but because it gives me reason to escape for a while the important but dreary role of housekeeper to my family.

While Mrs Lennox and Caroline take the conversation off into the arrangements of the fair, I stir sugar into my tea and nibble at a tiny, fussy little cake, all the while thinking of where I might go with my burden of pamphlets … not just the narrow Wynds where the children play in the dirt and dust, I think. Many little ones – too young yet for the harsh work of the factories – run off to the fresh air and open space of Glasgow Green with their friends, or scuttle around down by the harbour, often begging a coin here and there from cheerful passengers disembarking from or awaiting the steamers. My pulse quickens at the thought of these purposeful wanderings, though I have no expectation that I can persuade Lachlan to join me.

Now, if things were different, it would have been the perfect time to have the perfect companion with me…

Where is he? a whispering creeps into my mind, and I quickly shake myself, lest I am lost in the longing for my old, dear friend Will.

Blinking quickly, I look off out of the tall, wide window of the drawing room as a distraction – and instantly frown.

Outside, the front gate – which I carefully and respectfully closed behind me – is now open. And two figures are in the garden, part hidden behind the rose bush.

A gasp is strangled in my throat when I see a pair of familiar brown eyes lock on to mine … and then Lachlan turns and runs from the garden, followed by the scruffy person of his friend Alec, and with the accompanying bark of an unseen dog.

And there is worse to come, in this very room.

"…and I meant to tell you, Caroline dear: I think we may have new recruits to our cause!" Mrs Lennox is saying, quite unaware of the trespassers that have just left her property. "Yesterday, I made the acquaintance of two ladies in a tea room – a Mrs Palmer-Reeves and her daughter – who have taken lodgings in Glasgow for the summer."

The saucer I am holding tilts, nearly sending the

dainty cup flying. I straighten just in time, hoping Mrs Lennox does not notice.

"They have an estate somewhere in the Isles, but have come to the city as a diversion," Mrs Lennox carries on blithely, "and so I thought I might interest them in our charitable work!"

"Oh!" Caroline gasps, choking on the sip of tea that she has just taken.

"Caroline dear! Are you all right?" asks Mrs Lennox with concern.

I want to roar "No!"; I want to yell that the Laird's wife and daughter have not a good, kind bone in their bodies!

"Ah, I think that would cause some difficulty for Caroline," Ishbel answers in a more measured fashion, as she passes a lace-edged handkerchief to our friend. "*Mr* Palmer-Reeves was Caroline's guardian before she married, and it was ... not a *happy* relationship."

"My!" says Mrs Lennox. "Well, in that case, do not worry, Caroline dear. I shall say not a word to them, if I should see them about town."

Caroline, my sisters and myself, it is as if we are one ... all letting out a slow sigh of relief at Mrs Lennox's promise.

And I suppose that is that. There was a brief sighting of ghosts – too close, too real – but the door has been firmly shut on them.

And yet, even though we are settled in a room that is bright and rich with colour, I suddenly feel as if we four are scuttling, small creatures in the undergrowth, sensing the looming shadow of the sea eagle on the hunt above us.

CHAPTER 16

It is uncommonly warm, even with the light brushes of breeze that dance across the slapping surface of the busy river, cooling the crowds that mill about the harbour.

The pile of pamphlets in my hands is small now; I have been busy the last few days, handing them out between my chores to children at play in the dark, dank Wynds, racing around in packs at Glasgow Green, and now here at the harbourside.

Perhaps I can take a moment to rest, I think, hunching down against a pile of jute-wrapped lengths of what I think must be fabric, woven, dyed, packaged and awaiting their next journey, I suppose. To where, I wonder? North to the Highlands? South to England? Or further afield … to South Africa, perhaps? The colonies of Australia? Canada or America, even?

Impatiently, I shake my head to rid myself of whispers that lurk within my secret self, as I gaze about me at the hustle and bustle.

Wide-eyed passengers mix with weary porters; rough-speaking seamen pass top-hatted businessmen.

Glossy steamers moor upwind of ugly dredgers; stacked carts and solid ponies wait patiently next to sleek carriages pulled by equally sleek horses.

Warehouses sit with yawning-wide doors, as the next load is moved in or out; shipping offices keep their smart doors shut, till a customer arrives with the fare that will take them to New York, New Zealand, Nova Scotia.

I'm not certain of the time now, but we are all invited for supper at Samuel and Caroline's this evening. There'll be talk of Mrs Palmer-Reeves and Miss Kitty being somewhere about Glasgow, I am sure, but Samuel keeps reminding Caroline that there is no need for her to fear them; she is legally free of that family forever. Father has said similar to us: "Time has passed, and Mr Palmer-Reeves will have long forgotten nobodies like us, I am sure. And do not forget; Caroline is independently wealthy, *and* our friend. If ever the Laird found me and tried to press charges, Caroline's lawyer could raise the issue of what Mr Palmer-Reeves had planned for her future."

So we have shields for the ghosts, it seems. But it does not mean I do not carry a dread of bumping into them on the bustling city streets.

With a shiver, I think to look for the building Father is working on further down the docks, so that we could walk to Caroline and Samuel's apartments together.

Effie will make her own way, naturally, and Lachlan ... who knows if he will turn up at all, the way things stand. I fear Father will begin to lose his even temper with our brother, if things continue the way they are. For Lachlan sulks and talks to no one, is gruff when asked to do anything, and disappears whenever he can.

And I am so tired today because of Lachlan; the last few nights, I have been unable to sleep, wondering why he is so unreachable. I spoke to no one else of his peculiar actions the other day in Mrs Lennox's garden. Lachlan had sought me out later at home and told me he had thought better of coming, that Alec had persuaded him to be polite and accept the invitation, but that he had become too shy as he approached the villa. But something does not sit right here; Lachlan would not say why he and his friend did something so peculiar as hiding in the garden, and as for Alec, well, he does not strike me as a lad who cares much for politeness and manners.

My mind really is quite worn out with trying to fathom the truth of it. Before I try to give away the last of my pamphlets and attempt to find Father, I *could* just close my eyes and rest awhile, with the sun to bathe me and the chatter and clatter blurring, buzzing, fading all around me, till ... till...

I am scrambling up a rocky outcrop, lungs burning from the effort.

Heart pounding fit to burst, fingers stinging, ripped by stone.

Grey sea mist swirls around as I climb, like a sickly, wet cloak.

Above, I hear my unseen brother cry for help.

Below, I hear my sisters' voices, calling.

Calling my name, so mournfully.

As if I am lost.

So very lost.

Lost to *them*?

A wetness on my hand wakes me from my brief, unpleasant slumber.

"Patch?" I say in surprise, as I shake myself awake on finding my hand licked by a scratchy little tongue.

The dog wags his tail, nay, his whole *bottom*, in delight at finding me so unexpectedly. And now I delight at knowing my brother – a vital part of that dreadful dream I just had – is unexpectedly near too.

"Lachlan?" I mumble, pushing myself upright.

I glance around, trying to make out his spikes of rough, red hair in the milling crowds.

A smile forms on my lips as I suddenly settle on my brother – until I make out the shocking thing he is doing. For Lachlan is behind a casually sauntering young man, and appears to be slipping his hand into the man's coat pocket, unseen!

I swear, I have never moved so quickly in all my life.

With the remaining pamphlets scattered to the ground and the puzzled pup in my wake, I run like a girl possessed, as if Mother herself is with me, her energy in my very muscles and veins, doubling my speed.

"Oof! Ow!" yelps Lachlan, as I charge into him, my arms wrapping around his waist, spinning him clear away from the man and his coat before anything can be taken.

I am aware that the young man looks over his shoulder, laughing a little at the sight of what he must think to be squabbling, scrapping children. Better he thinks this, of course, than the truth of what *I* saw.

"What are you doing?" I hiss at Lachlan, only loud enough for my brother to hear. Though my words will no doubt be masked to those around, due to the frenzied barking of Patch.

"I – I – I am doing *nothing*!" Lachlan explodes, his face red, tears of anger and embarrassment threatening, I can see, like in those shared, dark days of ours in Mr Simpson's classroom.

"Do not lie to me, Lachlan!" I hiss again, raging at my little brother, though he is already taller than me.

But Lachlan continues to hold that he was doing nothing but strolling along the quayside with Alec and Patch, idly watching the river traffic. I know this to be far from the truth, since I see the dark head of Alec bob away with much haste into the crowd. If nothing was untoward, why would he not stay by his friend's side?

Lachlan's protestations continue in a similar fashion as I march him to Samuel and Caroline's apartments, his ire ebbing to a brooding silence by the time we arrive.

"Bridie, come on in! Hello there, Lachlan!" says Samuel, as he opens the door to us, and bends to ruffle Patch's ears.

I hesitate a little before ushering my brother in ahead of me. Samuel seems … odd. He is always friendly, of course, but today he is excited, agitated even. And it is most unusual for Ishbel not to answer the door, since that is naturally one of her duties.

"Come away in, do!" Samuel exclaims, waving us into the studio, rather than the drawing room. That is not so unusual; we are just as likely to take tea in here as in the drawing room, while Samuel shows us his latest work, whether that be a commissioned, posed portrait of a rich merchant, or some new, tender sketch of Caroline.

It must be said, though, it is quite unnerving to be in the room and see yourself mirrored back. The quick sketch Samuel did of me at the top of the Glas Crags, my black hair spinning and tangling at the wind's will, has now become a work-in-progress oil painting, fixed on an easel by the window. Drawings of Ishbel, Effie and myself are pinned to the walls, awaiting a future time when Samuel can translate them into something more. (I like the most finished of them, with a watercolour wash. It is the first time I can truly see the resemblance between myself and my sisters, as three sets of Mother's pale-grey eyes stare out of the page.)

"Is – is all quite well?" I ask warily, seeing that both Ishbel and Caroline are holding hands and looking most peculiar; smiling, and yet it is as if they have been caught in the midst of a delicate conversation, perhaps?

"We were going to wait till your father and Effie got here," Samuel chatters, "but I'm not sure we can hold in our news, can we, Caroline?"

"Indeed not, my dear," says Caroline, with no hat and veil here indoors to conceal the high feeling that makes her cheeks so very reddened. She almost meets my gaze, but then looks away sharply. Why?

Oh…

Immediately, I blush too. Are they about to tell us the *best* of news? That they are to have a child?

"I have had the most *splendid* offer," Samuel announces instead. "A bank in London has offered me a commission to paint the portraits of their partners. *All* of their partners. It will pay exceptionally well, and will employ me for the best part of a year, perhaps more!"

Foolishly, all I understand of this is that my first guess at their news was wrong. It takes my brother, sounding like the nervous child he once was, to ascertain the truth of what Samuel is telling us.

"You are leaving us?" he asks, with a crack in his voice.

"For just a year, I promise," says Samuel, grabbing Lachlan by the shoulders.

"To go to London?" I add, now that I regretfully understand what has been said. "Is this because of…"

"…the ghosts", I want to say, though no one else calls the human reminders of our past by this name. But Caroline understands my meaning surely enough.

"No," she says brightly, *lying*, I can tell. "It is just such a wonderful opportunity for Samuel!"

Yes, I am angry at the idea of our uncommon but wonderful family breaking up, but how can I blame Caroline? For perhaps was not the fate Mr Palmer-Reeves had planned for her as bad or worse than what might have happened to Father? Would I not run from the memories of it, if I was able?

"Perhaps you could come and visit us!" Samuel says as brightly as he can muster, now that he sees the effect the news has had on Lachlan and I. "We had actually hoped that we could tempt Ishbel to come with us, in fact…"

No, no, no! I cry inside, not able to bear the notion of being even more torn asunder.

"…but she has sadly declined," adds Caroline, her own expression a confusion of happiness and regret. "She does not wish to leave you all."

The hammering of my heart eases. Of *course* Ishbel would not wish to leave us, not after what we have been through together, I think to myself as I look to my sister, whose gaze has dropped to the floor. For my sisters and I, leaving Tornish meant we found how much we loved one another.

Samuel appears to be about to speak again, but there is a sudden, sharp cracking sound – one that startles the breath from my throat, it is so like the crack of a gunshot – till my senses accept it is just a knocking at the apartment door.

Father's rhythm of a knock.

Ishbel drops Caroline's hands and hurries to answer it.

Those of us left in the studio hear the heavy clunk of the door handle turning and the beginning of "Hello" leave Ishbel's lips – and then comes such a ragged scream!

We are all of us up and racing in an instant. Coming out of the bright room and into the duskier hallway, at first I make out Father catching hold of Ishbel as she faints. Then a figure behind him steps forward.

Which ghost made human is this? I fret. Till all at once, I recognise him.

"Fergus? Fergus Matheson?" I call out, scarce believing my eyes.

"Aye, Bridie," says the now bearded but still handsome young man in the doorway.

A quarter-hour passes until we are all settled and seated in the drawing room, with Effie now arrived, and Ishbel revived, though she is still shockingly pale and her eyes cannot be drawn from Fergus's face (I think she must have thought him his brother Donal, her favourite, when she first opened the door to him and Father).

"You bumped into each other at the harbour?" Effie is asking, catching up on the little she has so far missed.

"I was heading for the shipping office, when I saw the fine figure of your father," Fergus explains, turning the cap he holds in his hands. "I swear I have never been so glad to see anyone!"

"Is he not looking well?" says Father, patting Fergus firmly on the forearm, as if he cannot quite believe him solid and surviving, after the bad business on the island.

"Indeed," Samuel agrees heartily. His dealings with the Matheson brothers and George were few, but he has come to know everything of what happened leading up to our family's flight from Tornish. "Where have you been this last year?"

"Working on a large farm south of here," says Fergus, with a slow nod that seems to indicate that was a decent enough outcome for him, compared to what could have been. "And tomorrow I am to set off to Canada; there is plenty similar work there, and the chance, by and by, to have land of my own."

"My, my…" Father mutters thoughtfully. "I have read in the newspapers that America has passed a Homestead Act, so folk can have their own place there too, in the western territories."

LITTLE BIRD FLIES

At that turn in the conversation, I sense whispers begin to whirl in the back of my mind, but I will not let myself listen to them.

"What of Donal? And George?" I demand, a little too loud, a little too impolitely, I think, but what does it matter?

Is it not what we *all* wish to know, especially Ishbel and Effie? My sisters may have accepted their new circumstances with good cheer, but it does not mean that they do not have their times of wondering and worrying about their former beaus. I see both now stiffen at my question, holding themselves steady for whatever answer Fergus might have for them.

"George was headed towards Aberdeen when we parted," Fergus explains. "There are fishing fleets all up and down the north-east coast, and he knew he could easily get work that way."

"And – and did he? Is he well?" Effie asks nervously.

"I suppose so," Fergus answers her, twisting his cap in agitation, aware of the effect of his words.

Indeed, with no set plan or place to settle in, how would Fergus find how George fared? And what a tragedy that is. One person moves here, another there, and family or fond friends find themselves parted, lost to each other forever, very likely. Oh, I cannot bear to think how very quickly and easily that terrible loss can happen…

"And Donal?" I hear Ishbel ask, in a very soft, barely-there voice.

"Ah, now he is well," Fergus says more surely, and I see Ishbel's tight shoulders slacken at the good news.

But then Fergus seems to stumble in his conversation, as if he is uncertain how to continue. It is left to Father to tell Ishbel of her intended's fate.

"Donal got work on the same farm as Fergus," he says, reaching over to take Ishbel's hands in his. "But he left Scotland this spring, bound for the diamond mines of South Africa. Fergus received a letter from him last month, saying he is quite set with work, and … and is recently wed."

Wed.

A small word that is like a bruising blow to the chest to Ishbel, who crumples where she sits, her head bowed.

So now both my sisters have knowledge – though it hurts rather than salves them – of the boys they cared for. What of mine? My dear friend, if not sweetheart?

"Is Will still on Tornish? Or is his family gone from there now?" I question Fergus, thinking of the Laird's intention to push *all* the tenants from Tornish as soon as was possible.

Will: the one "ghost" of my past that I would dearly love to see, and to see made real.

"Sorry, Bridie – I have no news at all from the island. I have not dared send a letter, and seen no one from that part of the world for this last year," Fergus says ruefully. "I had hoped your Father might have news for *me*!"

Father shakes his head slowly, for we too have worried over the danger of getting word to friends back on the island, in case anyone should intercept the correspondence and cause trouble for our friends.

There is a thoughtful silence for a moment, which is broken by the hiccuping sobs of Ishbel.

"I had better go, I think," said Fergus, getting up as if to take his leave.

In the flurry of refusals that follow, with Father and Samuel and Caroline insisting Fergus stay, my sisters and I sit quiet in our own reveries.

Yes, I am as unsettled as Ishbel and Effie, though for a different reason.

Fergus's unexpected visit is over, but it has made the whispers of my secret self grow ever louder and more insistent by the minute.

CHAPTER 17

I marvel at the marionettes.

These wooden dolls seem so animated and of human form that I can scarce believe they are not the fabled fairies and Little Folk of the Highlands brought to life!

They are painted in bright colours, dressed in brighter costumes still. And by way of their wires, they are made to talk and act in a manner that is quite charming.

Every child sitting on the grass of the neat garden square is open-mouthed in wonder, when they are not laughing loudly at the foolish antics of the puppets, that is. The message Mrs Lennox wants them all to know – about the evils of drink – has not yet become clear, but the story will lead to that soon, I am sure.

With the audience so entertained, I think to step away, to help clear things at the refreshment tables. For there – as well as at the coconut shy, the skittles run, the hoop-throwing and other such games and diversions – all is quite quiet, now that the marionette show works its magic.

"Ha! They are like a huddle of dirty little rats, are they not, Mother?"

At the sound of the familiar voice, my weaker foot lets me down, and I stumble.

This ghost from my past, her mean-spirited words take me back to the first time I heard her speak, on Beltane evening a year past, when her honey-dripped voice mocked the island children and their traditions. The night she gave such a queer smile when the old Laird died, bless his soul; a smile I realised later told of a dark and greedy heart.

"Yes, quite, Kitty!" I hear Mistress Palmer-Reeves purr in agreement.

They are both here, then? But Mrs Lennox promised she would not invite them. I suppose they were told about the show, innocently enough, by some of the other ladies helping out today.

"*Why* this Mrs Lennox thinks she make a difference to the lives of such riff-raff I do not know," I hear the Laird's awful wife prattle on. "An urchin will *never* be more than an urchin."

And *this* urchin can bear it no longer.

I am shaking as if the so-called fine ladies are *actual* spectres; ones who will wrap their chill arms around me and drag me back to a dark and frightening time I wish to forget.

In the normal way of things, I might think myself

small but strong, but not right now. Suddenly I am as weak as I have ever been, and there is such a rushing in my ears and a blackness in my head as I turn and race towards the table of women who are assisting today.

But among them, where are my sister and Caroline, or even Mrs Lennox?

Perhaps my panic has made me blind; I stare frantically, but cannot make out any of them in the blur of puffed skirts, helping hands and nodding heads in neat hats.

And so my panic balloons, and all I am able to do is run; run away from the grassy square as fast as I am able, though I know not where to go, where I might feel safe.

I find myself hurtling across the top of the road where Mrs Lennox lives when I hear something familiar…

A bark. And another.

A volley of barks, in fact – followed by a terrible howl and whimpering.

"Patch!" I call out, and hurry down towards some confused gathering of dark figures by Mrs Lennox's gate, one still with his leg cocked, as if he has just delivered a sharp kick.

Our little dog; he is a way away from the group, wriggling in pain on his side. "Patch!!"

"Steady! Be still!" I hear one of the figures order.

But in this chaos of figures, my attention is on our pup; I fall to the dusty ground by his side, where he whimpers and yet strives to give my hand a fond lick.

"Is it yours, miss?" a gruff voice asks, and I look up to see there are three men close by me on the pavement; two policemen who hold tight an angry, clench-jawed older lad between them. It is one of the policemen who questions me.

The strange thing is, *all* three of them look familiar!

A moment's confused thought provides me with some answers. The two policemen: they had stopped by the fair round the corner very recently indeed, to check that all was well – and have a sup of fruit punch while they were at it.

But why the wretched, angry creature between the police should be known to me I cannot say…

"Yes, yes – the dog is mine!" I say haltingly, as I try to gently pick up Patch, now whimpering pitifully. "What has happened here?"

An older, white-haired gent answers from the front garden of the house next door, with his shaken wife beside him, clinging to his arm.

"Your dog is quite the hero!" says the old gentleman. "This lout had broken into Mrs Lennox's house, but your dog's barking alerted us to the act, and when I came out here, I was lucky enough to see these policemen at the top of the street and call out to them."

"We caught him coming out the window, his pockets full," says the other policeman. "Your dog might be little, but it is a fighter and would not let go this brute's ankle while we caught hold of him."

"Aye, and it got clout for its trouble," says the older gent, with a shake of his head. "Pity it was not a bigger sort who could do more damage to the likes of *him*. Or better still, that it were two dogs, and one could have given chase to the fellow's imp of an accomplice, that ran away so speedily!"

The older lad launches a gob of spit in the direction of the white-haired gent and his wife, and gets a thump on the chest with a truncheon for his trouble.

"We'd better get him to the cells," one of the policemen explains to the clearly disgusted gent. "Can you alert the owner of the property, sir, and tell her to come to the station?"

"*I* know Mrs Lennox," I say hurriedly. "And she is just at the fair you have come directly from!"

It is my nature to think to go, but my movement seems to cause pain to Patch and he whimpers more terribly.

"Just on the square, there? Let *me* fetch her!" says the old gent, as the policemen wrestle the lad off. "You attend to this little hero of yours…"

With my head reeling at so many turns of events, I carefully walk into Mrs Lennox's garden and slowly sit down on her front doorstep, all the while cradling the shivering bundle in my lap.

"I think I have seen you before, my dear," the elderly

lady says, wringing her hands agitatedly as her husband hurries off.

"My sister is maid to Mrs Lennox," I tell her.

"Ah yes, a lovely girl she is," I hear the woman say. "Only the other day I was chatting to her and…"

The lady's words drift on, but something in the bushes of the garden, the tiniest of movements, makes me freeze.

Someone is huddled under the rose bush.

A pair of desperate, pleading eyes gaze up at me.

A shaking finger is placed to pinched lips drained of colour, begging for silence.

Now all is clear, as if a grey sea mist rises to let the shifting shapes take form.

The older lad held between the policemen, that brute who broke into Mrs Lennox's house … I saw him once before! This week, in fact, at the harbour. My brother had his hand slipped in that grown lad's coat pocket. And the "imp" that was mentioned – the accomplice that got away – it was Alec, wasn't it?

The brute and Alec; they *knew* that this particular house would be empty of its owner and staff this afternoon, because there was a *third* accomplice, who told them so.

And that third accomplice was my own brother.

"Let me go and see if I have some warm blanket for that poor wee scrap," I hear the old lady neighbour say.

"I won't be long."

As she shuffles off, the tatters of my recent daydream drift unsettlingly in my head. What I face here is as hard and sharp and difficult as any perilous rocky climb.

But I have not the time to dwell on dreams and difficulties; distant, higher-pitched voices of ladies alert me to the fact that Mrs Lennox, Caroline, my sisters and all manner of outraged committee members of the Temperance Movement will be here shortly.

And all that comes to me is the words I regularly speak to Mother at Eliza Garnett's angel: "I will *always* protect him, I promise."

With a heavy heart, I glare at Lachlan and hiss, "Go! Out through the back garden – hurry!"

For the first time in a long time, my now sobbing little brother does as he is told, scampering on his hands and knees like a dog himself, and not a moment too soon.

"Oh, dear me! Dear me!" Mrs Lennox calls out, as she hurtles through the garden gate.

"Are you all right?" Ishbel calls out, rushing to me, quickly followed by Caroline.

Behind them, a gaggle of women chatter in concern, flapping around like geese bothered by a buzzard.

And standing outside on the pavement, drawn by the excitement no doubt, I see my ghosts – Mistress Palmer-Reeves and Miss Kitty.

LITTLE BIRD FLIES

And it is the strangest thing; they may be dressed in finery and flounces, but the older and the younger woman look washed-out and woebegone. The dullness of being wealthy on a bleak island has made them sick at heart, I think. Tornish's quiet beauty will have passed them by, as they struggled with their fools' umbrellas in the storms of winter and the blustering breezes of spring alike.

They'll have watched the island empty of folk at the Laird's orders, becoming more of a solitary prison with every cheerful, good family that left.

The Mistress and Miss Kitty are broken and bowed, no matter how they try to retain their pride, and … and I fear them no more.

I vow I shall fear no more ghosts of the past.

Not when there have been everyday demons chasing my brother, under our noses, all this time.

CHAPTER 18

Always, *always* Father is gentle-spoken with us.

But not today.

"Stand straight!" he orders Lachlan, who is trembling so much he can barely remain upright.

Ishbel goes to comfort our brother, and Father gives her such a glower she sits back in her chair, chastised. From my own chair on the other side of the room, I see Effie reach for her hand.

"So let me be clear, son," Father carries on, stroking his beard in agitation rather than thoughtfulness as he stands at the fireplace. "First, you learn from Alec how to steal apples and pies and suchlike from street vendors?"

Though Lachlan stutters and tremors, the whole truth is unfolding. Not just of the awful event at Mrs Lennox's house this afternoon, but of events that came before.

"Y— yes, Father," Lachlan answers nervously, tears and snot streaming down his face.

"And then he encourages you to act like a pauper and beg from rich folk?" Father continues, his brown eyes so terribly dark.

"Yes, though I had no talent for it!" Lachlan says, as if his lack of success will absolve him. "One gentleman even laughed at me, saying I was too hale and hearty to be a pauper. But then Alec told me I must make people pity me by—"

Lachlan stops, his wet, pale face flushing with some shameful secret.

"Pity you how?" Father says sharply. "Speak up!"

Lachlan's head drops, so that his chin hits his chest before he speaks again. "He told me I should act as if I were a cripple. He told me it would be easy; I only had to mimic my sister's walk and weakness…"

I take a sharp, gasping breath. I have become almost used to the stares and remarks of strangers in this city, and have made myself quite hardened to them. But for my own brother to do such a thing!

"I tried just once, Bridie," Lachlan bursts out, looking over at me pleadingly, "but I could not bring myself to—"

"And *yet*," Father interrupts him, "after that, after Alec introduced you to his 'good friend' Skinner, you next let *him* teach you the ways of pickpocketing?"

Skinner. We have come to know the last name of this lout that broke into Mrs Lennox's home, but not his first. It seems Lachlan has never known that either.

"Y—yes," stammers Lachlan. "Skinner would walk in a crowd, and I was expected to come up behind him unseen, and — and try to take something from his pocket. But I had no talent for that either. Even Bridie saw me fail at it."

Now Father fixes me with such a look as I have never seen him give me before.

"You knew of this, Bridie, and you didn't think to tell me?"

His other hand rests on the mantle, fingers drumming a slow, heavy rhythm.

"Lachlan kept assuring me I was mistaken," I tell Father, feeling shaken myself at his quiet rage. "But I was stern with him, talking about the folly of such a thing, whether he was guilty of it or not. I thought that might be enough, and be a lesson learned…"

"Well, it seems your guidance was for nothing, doesn't it, Bridie?" says Father. "Because young Lachlan here *did* have a talent for something. He was good at helping a criminal rob the goods of a fine and noble lady like Mrs Lennox!"

We have already heard how this Skinner had ambitions for his criminal apprentices. A housebreak it was to be, once Alec had alerted their keen tutor of the fine homes Lachlan had connection with.

It made us all shudder to hear that Samuel and

Caroline's apartments were to have a similar visitation one day soon, if Skinner had not been apprehended as he was earlier.

"A fine and noble lady who is also your sister's employer, Lachlan," Father roars, making Patch whimper in his pained sleep on the rug. "What have you to say for yourself, eh?"

"I told you already, Skinner *made* me do it!" Lachlan splutters and cries.

"And you had no conscience?" Father roars again. "This young man can direct you to do terrible things to people who have shown us only kindness? You did not find it possible to refuse this monster's requests?"

"When I first knew Alec, he would give me things: sweets, a penknife, a magnifying glass," Lachlan says. "And then he said it was bad luck not to give him things in return. But I had nothing! So he said the luck would be changed if I did things for him. For Skinner. And if I did not…"

"So you believed this — this threat, this idle superstition?" Father says, throwing a dark glance at Effie, as if her talk of fairies and sprites and broken Beltane cakes on the island had made Lachlan's thinking weak.

"Yes, at first I did, Father! And then, when I tried to say I had done enough, Skinner held his knife to me," says Lachlan, his whole body quivering as he holds up his hands, as if to beg forgiveness. "He told me he would cut Patch's throat if I did not do as he said. And he would not stop at that; for Alec told him I had three sisters..."

Father's rage is instantly stilled; Ishbel and Effie clasp their hands to their mouths in shock.

But at this awful moment I have seen something quite clear, and in my rush to reach my brother my chair tumbles and clatters to the floor behind me.

"Here!" I say to Lachlan, grabbing his outstretched hands.

He was not begging, he was showing. Showing the malicious marks of a knife carefully and cruelly dragged across the skin, several times on each wrist.

Oh, how did we not notice this before?

We sisters, so busy about our days, worrying about ghosts that did not matter, none of us took the time to see the secret signs of the trouble our brother was in.

But *I* bear the guilt most, as *I* am supposed to take care of him. Is that not my job? Is that not the promise I made to Mother too?

Lachlan collapses gratefully into my arms.

His despairing cries are so loud, it takes my sisters' earnest shouts and the slam of the door to realise Father is gone.

An hour passes.

LITTLE BIRD FLIES

The room is so very quiet.

The mantle clock ticks, the dog snuffles in its pained sleep by the fire, and sometimes a sob can be heard from the big bed in the corner where Lachlan retreated, curling himself in a ball while Ishbel sits minding him.

Other than that, it is as if Ishbel, Effie and myself are holding our breath, coiled as cold metal springs as we await Father's return.

When he first left, we three did chatter like troubled starlings on a rooftop, wondering what Father was set on doing. Finding Alec, and berating him for dragging Lachlan into this dark world of thievery? Or doing *worse* to him?

But our chatter slowed and shushed to this current, shared silent dismay.

And silence is my enemy, for it gives voice to the whispers that I keep so deep hidden.

Here comes one now, whirling its soft, urgent words into my mind: *Oh, where are you, Will?*

My, how my secret self yearns yet for my best friend! How I would love to run away with him to the Glas Crags, to shake off this dark episode and laugh with him and let him tease me as we clamber. Then we two could gaze together at the twinned land and sea, at the gulls that dip and dive between them.

And what of the other whisper? I think it also wants to be heard.

I was never meant…

But a long awaited sound disturbs the moment.

"Listen – it is him!" says Effie, looking up at the door now that the thud and creak of the stairs announce Father's return.

Effie and I both rise as he walks in and shuts the door more quietly than he did when he left.

The black-edged rage has left Father, I am relieved to see. Though his look – it is so very like that night a whole year ago, when he came back from his doomed meeting with the Laird.

"Father, where have you been?" asks Ishbel.

"To a pub," he announces, making us all startle with surprise.

Father may have a bottle of whisky in the house for special occasions, or for medicinal use, but he does not frequent bawdy public houses.

"I did not go to drink my sorrows away, though that was tempting," he says ruefully, as he walks over to the dresser. "I went to ask around about this Skinner character. And sure enough, he is known – even by hardened types – to be a very bad lot. From what was said about him, and the sorts he associates with, Lachlan is in an unfortunate situation."

"In danger, you mean?" I ask, though I know my question will frighten my brother – who sure enough curls himself tighter, and whimpers to rival the pup.

"Yes," Father says simply. "I think it is very likely that Skinner will tell in court of his accomplices, in a bid to lighten his own guilt in the matter."

"Oh, Father! What is to be done?" says Effie, her eyes brimming with frightened tears. "What will happen to Lachlan? And what of my position with Mrs Lennox when this is known? And Ishbel's when Samuel and Caroline find out they were to be victims? Are we ruined, *all* of us?"

"My loves, I think we must consider our future – and I fear it is not here," Father announces plainly. "Perhaps it never was. We're folk of the land, after all, not the city…"

As he talks, Father reaches up for Mother's tin box, which is hidden on top of the dresser, pressed far back against the wall so as not to be seen. "… and I think now is the time to use our money to—"

"NO!" comes a sudden yell, and Lachlan hurls himself off the bed in one bound, launching himself at Father and pulling frantically at the arm that is tugging open the lid of the box.

For a heartbeat there, I presume my brother so bound up in his remorse and regret that he is not thinking clearly. That the true, sweet boy that he is cannot bear another desperate dash and difficult new start.

And then I see – we *all* see – what is in the box…

Nothing.

Nothing at all.

Effie is right; the MacKerrie family are truly, truly ruined.

Unless, unless…

CHAPTER 19

Flutter and flap, flutter and flap…

The flag on top of the pole jigs around, mirroring the skittish bundles of cloud in today's blue July sky.

"Oh … *ohhhh*…" comes a groan.

I turn away from viewing the flag, and the giant black funnel that looms above, alongside the masts from this steamship's former sailing past.

"There now," I say gently, as I rub Lachlan's back with my good hand. With my other I wave to whoever can make me out on the quayside, if they can make me out at all among the other departing passengers here on the deck.

Poor lamb. Lachlan leans over the polished wood rail, holding tight to it as if that will save him from the treacherous sway beneath his feet. We have been on board the *Ailsa Craig* for no time at all; we have barely begun our journey along the Clyde. How will he manage a fortnight's travel if he is sick already?

"Can you – can you see him?" I hear Lachlan mutter.

"He is close by," I assure my brother, glancing along the deck to where Father talks now to some official of the Anchor Line, trying to fix on the exact whereabouts of the berths promised to families, in the cheap steerage accommodation where most folk of our class will spend the two-week voyage.

"No, I meant *Patch*!" says Lachlan, lifting his head, though the effort of it appears to make his head – or his stomach – spin all the more.

I peer at the receding quayside and the large gathering of folk there – and can still make out our little party of leave-takers among them; it is quite easy to spot Caroline's pretty pink hat and matching gloves as she waves, and of course Patch is the light shape cradled carefully against Samuel's wine-coloured velvet coat.

For Patch is not to come with us: he is too poorly to make much of a journey. We hope his little body heals soon, and he will have the best chance of that now. Being such a hero, saving Mrs Lennox's precious things as he did, Patch's reward is to spend the rest of his days – however many he may have left – lying on expensive Persian rugs by any of Mrs Lennox's fireplaces that he chooses.

"I can see him; he looks just grand," I lie to Lachlan, whose head dips down again as he is caught in a wave of illness.

"Oh, no! *Look*, Bridie ... Ishbel will be cross at the

mess I have made!" my brother suddenly wails, and I see the sick on his new-polished boots.

"She will not!" I say cheerfully. "And how ever will she see the state of them?"

"Oh, yes," Lachlan answers with a frown, then risks lifting his head enough to look in the direction of Caroline and Samuel, since Ishbel stands between them, her cheerful, sky-blue dress quite clear there, among the dark suits and jackets in the crowd. We are too far away to fix on her lovely face, but I can imagine her chin held high, her grey eyes watching, watching, till the ship is quite gone from view.

It is true; my elder sister is not to travel with us.

She is to make an escape of sorts herself, heading to London after all with Caroline and Samuel. And how could Father try to persuade her otherwise, when her heart is set on it? For Ishbel is quite the city girl now, and the thought of living on some little farm again in some unknown landscape in the vast expanse of America is not to her liking.

Also, Father could hardly protest, since it was Caroline who came to our rescue, when my family thought no rescue was possible.

"Just as your girls came to mine," Caroline told him, when she and Samuel followed me back to our door, after I ran to tell them of our troubles.

When Father opened Mother's tin box two nights

ago, we found out that Lachlan had not yet told us *all* of the terrible crimes Alec and Skinner had forced upon him. After once innocently – *foolishly* – boasting of the money we had stored, the two lads were quite fiercely determined that my brother should bring it to them. And Lachlan had lived with the ugly guilt of that deed many weeks now, always dreading discovery…

"This is just a loan, now, Caroline," Father had insisted, taking the money that would be enough to purchase our fares to New York, as well as start us off in our new life in some quieter territory beyond, wherever that may be. Father was not yet sure of our final destination; only knowing vaguely from his newspaper of the Homestead Act recently passed in America, and the chance for hardworking farming folk to have land of their own with no lairds and no masters to answer to.

New York.

West, at last.

Can you believe it?

It all felt like a dream, a muddled imagining of mine, till just a few minutes ago, as the ropes were untied and the ship began to creak and move off, its engine growling.

"We'll miss the Glasgow Fair, won't we, Bridie?" Lachlan mutters sorrowfully as I dab at his mouth with a handkerchief. He sounds like any shallow-minded child who is not allowed some great treat, or perhaps like a young boy who wants to think of silly things, and not linger on sadness that might hurt too sorely.

"Indeed," I agree, wishing I could more clearly make out the hazy figures of our darling Ishbel, and Caroline and Samuel.

"All of the city will be gathering tomorrow, to see the entertainments," my brother says wistfully, turning his head away from the harbour crowds and toward the Green, upcoming on the riverbank, where the fair is always held.

"Well, it was the same with Queen Victoria, was it not?" I remind him, straining hopelessly for one last glance of Ishbel as the crowd blurs. "We missed Her Majesty coming to the island, and we will miss the fair. But think of the wonders to come … a whole new land of them!"

A sudden whispering comes to me, blown on the breeze, or called by the seagulls that drift upriver; but I have too much on my mind to listen to them.

"Look – the Necropolis," Lachlan says suddenly, nodding his head weakly in the direction of the rising land that is *just* visible beyond the packed rooftops of the city. "Can you see Mother's angel from here, Bridie?"

"No, but it is there," I say softly, my eyes fixed to the faraway jumbled glint of white marble and grey granite headstones.

Yes, it is a regret that there was not time enough to

visit Eliza Garnett's grave before we left, just as I could not take my leave of Mother's true resting place in the churchyard on Tornish. But Mother is always where *we* are, wherever that may be. And wherever I am bound for, there will always be a hill or tree or some beautiful place where I can talk to her.

"Do you think she is very sad that we are parted from one another?" asks Lachlan, most forlornly.

"Remember what Mother would say: 'It is what it is'…" I remind my brother, with as bright a smile as I can muster.

Lachlan blinks back at me and says, "I did not mean *Mother*; I meant Effie."

Effie.

Oh, darling Effie… I do my best to keep my smile strong, and look back at the quayside for her. Not that I have much hope of seeing her; she vanished from the others a while back. Perhaps it was all too sad for her. Perhaps at the last minute, she regretted her decision to stay with Mrs Lennox, who so wonderfully forgave my brother, even though Effie chose to go and tell her all that had happened in the most clear and brutally honest way she could.

But I know in my heart that Effie will not have changed her mind. For the city suits our middle sister as much as – no, even *more* than – Ishbel. The bossy, strait-laced girl so wrapped up in superstition … she was left behind on Tornish, leaving way for this softer, happier girl who blossomed in Mrs Lennox's bright, bustling household.

And I must not dwell on my strange nightmare here, the one that came to me when I fell into a slumber at the harbour, for my sisters are *not* lost to me. We may be gone from each other, but Ishbel and Effie are happy, and searching for their own dreams.

Good dreams.

And we have promised to send each other letters often. Father, Lachlan and I will pass through New York quickly, and as soon as we are settled – wherever that might be – I will write to them both to let them know where we are. Where our new home is. Ha!

"Is that not her?" Lachlan suddenly says, glancing back towards the harbour's edge and pointing at some particular figure he has spied. "Is that not her lilac dress? Bridie?"

I do not answer straightaway for two reasons.

First, it is because my heart races too fast, knowing the frantically waving person who has climbed upon an empty flat cart – the better to see and be seen – can be no one else but Effie. Far away as she is, the flame red of her hair is distinct as a match lit in the dusk.

And second, because there is the figure of a lad beside her. He waves too, with both arms. For a heartbeat, it reminds me of that hazy moment in Father's rowboat, when I imagined Will bidding me farewell from the top of the Glas Crags…

Where are you, Will? the whispering asks, as I laugh to myself at the sheer madness of my thoughts. Of course that is not Will. Of course it is just a boy, waving to some family member or friend who – like Lachlan and I – is arranged along the wooden railings in this raggedy, hopeful yet heart-sore line.

But would that not be another strange thing? Just as last year my family sailed from Tornish, missing Queen Victoria as she sailed in, what if I left Glasgow, while Will Beaton and his *own* folks arrived?

Still, what does it serve me to think of that fancy?

As I lean shoulder to shoulder with Lachlan and wave as hard and heartily as I am able in Effie's direction, I finally let my secret self speak the other whisper. The one I have long turned myself deaf to. For now – here on the deck of this ship bound for the horizon, for America, I am free to hear it said.

Listen, it tells me, as I take a final breath of smoky Glasgow air. *Listen.*

I was never meant to be here, in the city, in the east.

I was always destined to head westwards.

And now, on drifting, dancing winds, I'll go.

On this ship, if not on the wing.

For I am Little Bird,

And I *will* fly.

CASTLE GARDEN
EMIGRANT
LANDING DEPOT,
NEW YORK

CHAPTER 20

There is talk all around us.

Talk in languages that are soft and songlike or fast and jagged. Some are made up of hard-sounding words that hammer together like wood upon wood.

The folk that speak these languages are milling in their hundreds, if not thousands, here in the vast, round hall.

All of us are equally matched in exhaustion and eagerness, though small details of our clothing mark us out as quite unlike one another. The plaid shawl tied around my shoulders and chest speaks of Scotland. But what of the girls and their mother that sit on the bench in front? What country do their floral patterned headscarves signify? And the men in the heavy fur coats and hats; how cold is their old homeland that they dress like bears?

I am shaken from my thoughts as Lachlan tugs a corner of my shawl over his eyes. He lies curled on the bench beside me, his head in my lap. My brother wore himself out on the deck of the ship, yelling, jumping, laughing as the whole of New York grew nearer, larger, a dream or a story made real at last. But the queues for the tugboats that were to ferry us from the ship to Castle Garden, the queues to get into the building, the queues to answer questions about where we had come from, how our health was, to register our names, to leave our luggage, to buy food… All these queues, the crush of strangers, they have tired him to the point of desperation. So I told him to shut out the people and this place as best he can till his mind stills.

My own mind, however, delights in it all. While Father is off in another queue, exchanging our pounds, crowns and shillings for dollars, dimes and cents, I am more than content to sit here and stare about me as I stroke my brother's head. And I stare not only at my fellow travellers, wondering of their pasts and their futures. I stare up and around at the Emigrant Depot itself, which is not the factory-like building I had imagined it to be. With its tall, supporting columns and ornate ceiling, it has a likeness to a great cathedral. But then, with the seated balcony that swoops around its circular walls, it reminds me of the posters I saw of music halls back in Glasgow.

Ah, now there is something new to marvel at. A woman has begun to sing, in such a loud, pure voice … but so high a sound she makes! I have never heard the like of it before, each note soaring and dancing in the clear air above the heads of the crowds. The language of it I do not know, but it is so very lovely it hardly matters.

I am not the only one to find myself entranced. The rush and babble of countless conversations quietens as everyone glances about for the singer among us.

"Who is that?" asks Lachlan, sitting up now that the woman's voice has cast such a spell.

"I do not know," I reply, narrowing my eyes as if it will help me see her.

"*Sie ist da, siehst du? Ja?*" says the lady sitting next to me, whose baby sleeps blissfully in a basket on her lap.

I do not know her words, but their meaning is clear, especially as her finger jabs towards a mob of folk who are parting, clearing a space around a small, stout woman whose person and dress is unremarkable, though her voice is like that of an angel.

"*Vöglein, was singst du so laut? Warum, warum?*" the lady with the baby trills softly along with the woman in the crowd.

I turn to smile at her, but perhaps she sees me frown a little, unsure why the woman is singing, uncertain why this beautiful thing is happening.

"English?" asks the lady.

I do not correct her. She talks about my language (well, *one* of them), not the country of my birth.

"Yes," I tell her.

LITTLE BIRD FLIES

"Castle Garden – this was a very famous concert hall once," she tells me. "Jenny Lind sang here."

I frown again.

"You do not know of Jenny Lind?" the lady says in obvious surprise. "She was the greatest operatic singer in the world. They called her 'The Nightingale'. Kings, queens, presidents, they would come to see her perform."

"So the woman mimics this famous singer?" I ask.

"Yes. She is *wünderbar ja?*" she says with a smile, slipping back into her own language. "And this song is so very pretty. 'The Bird's Song' it is called. In English, she is saying…"

The lady pauses, tuning in to the woman in the crowd, and then sings snatches I can understand.

"Sweet bird, why so loudly you sing? Ah, why! Ah, why!
I sing, I sing, I sing but know not why.
Sweet bird, your little heart seems glad. Ah, why! Ah, why!
I sing while life is given to me, careless if any hear or see, I sing!"

I smile to myself, for here I am, a Little Bird listening to the song of The Nightingale.

And now I am here in America, my little heart is glad, and I sing.

ACKNOWLEDGEMENTS

I'm lucky enough to call two places home: London, where I've lived for many years with my Scottish husband and English daughter (and lots of cats!) and Scotland, where I was born and brought up. Returning to Scotland means visiting our families in the cities of Aberdeen and Dundee, but whenever we can, we take off and become tourists, soaking up the spectacular scenery of the countryside and coasts.

These getaways remind me so much of my childhood. My parents weren't very adventurous when it came to travelling, so summer meant a week in a caravan here or a day trip in the car there, all fairly close to home. But I loved it; the drama of the mountains, forests and lochs, the ancient castles steeped in stories. (And I really liked the regular stops for chips and ice-cream too!)

Sadly, Mum and Dad aren't around to thank personally, but I still owe them one for those excellent outings around Scotland when I was growing up.

As for research, I read a ton of fascinating books for this project, including *Highland Folk Ways* by I.F.Grant, who set up the amazing Highland Folk Museum in Kingussie, near Aviemore. Do go, if you ever get the chance – it's an outdoor museum comprised of different historic Scottish buildings, from blackhouses to school rooms to sweet shops. It's even been used as location for the hugely popular "Outlander" series!

But while books about the people and places of the region were invaluable, I really needed the input of one particular person to make sure I was getting my Highlands and Islands references as authentic as they could be, and that's the multi-talented and gorgeous Gaelic-speaking Mairi Kidd. Thanks for all your incredibly useful comments and pointers, Mairi!

I'd also like to thank my lovely, long-time friend Louise, who has always been my moan-listener, motivator and personal cheerleader when it comes to all things book-ish (and life-ish).

Then there's Sheena, Martin and Ruby, friends who years ago invited me and my family to visit the beautiful island of Ulva, near Mull. Although Tornish is a fictional island, I think there's definitely a hint of Ulva in there.

Lastly, a huge thank you goes to my husband Tom, who always told me I should tell this tale, and of course to Kirsty Stansfield and Kate Wilson at Nosy Crow, who read Little Bird's story and helped her to fly...

SCAN THIS QR CODE TO READ MORE ABOUT THE INSPIRATION BEHIND LITTLE BIRD FLIES